Writing Fiction

The Top 100 Best Strategies For Writing Fiction Stories

By Blaine Hart
Copyright © 2015

Check Out all My Books and Audio Books
at: www.LordHartRules.com

Table of Contents

Introduction

I want to thank you and congratulate you for downloading the book, "Writing Fiction: The Top 100 Best Strategies for Writing Fiction Stories."

Fiction is a wonderful way to forget about the real world and experience another world for a while. Many people enjoy reading fiction tales from the time they are old enough to read until they are so old they can barely see anymore. Not only do a lot of people enjoy reading fiction, some also enjoy writing it. If it weren't for the fiction writers in the world, there would be no great stories to escape from reality with! Do you dream of one day writing a fiction story that the whole world will enjoy? Then, look no further, because this book can help you discover how to unlock your inner creative genius and write a solid, well-structured fiction narrative.

Like any other creative task, fiction writing can be daunting and overwhelming. Writing a book may look easy but, as you soon will discover, the process consists of a multitude of complex components. Many people dive immediately into writing, expecting a book to flow automatically from the pen, only to discover how complicated can be. Without help, you can easily give up in despair.

Many skills are necessary if you want to write a decent book. You'll need to know how to write detailed descriptions and readable dialogue that pushes your plot forward. You must know how to portray believable and lovable characters that your readers will bond with quickly. Most essential but least intuitive, you will have to master the art of showing, instead of telling. Successful fiction writing also requires a solid, carefully structured plot containing unexpected twists and turns as well as a well-thought-out suspense-building strategy. In all, fiction writing calls for a great deal of planning, preparation, research, and trial-and-error perseverance, along with other things we will discuss throughout this book.

Have you dreamed of becoming the next Stephen King, Stephanie Meyer, Dan Brown or another favorite author? While this level of success in fiction writing is extremely difficult to achieve, the rewards are priceless and the hard work certainly pays off. The best way to set yourself up for success in such a challenging industry is to learn the ins and outs of how fiction writing really works. The better you're equipped to write a fiction story, the better are your chances of writing a best-seller.

This book contains proven steps and strategies to help you be successful in your fiction writing. You will discover the best ways to prepare yourself for writing and the best genres to write for. You will learn how to cover all the story "basics" so your book will attract the right audience. You will find ways to develop breakthrough characters, how to write compelling dialogue, how to use a variety of literary techniques to push your plot forward, how to develop a great plot, and much, much more.

Feeling like you're coming down with a case of writer's block? No worries. In this book you will discover ways to overcome writer's block and see how you can develop an idea from almost anything. There are a wide variety of fiction writing strategies waiting for you in the following pages. The more books you can write and sell, the higher your chances for success. So let's get started!

Chapter 1: Before You Write

So you've got a great idea and you're feeling inspired to finally start writing your book. You sit down at your computer, open up a blank document and just start typing away as fast as you can, right? Think again. While many people imagine it is plausible to just do that, there is actually one very important step you should take if you want to be successful. That step is **preparation**. Preparation is an important part of accomplishing anything, not just writing. Athletes prepare themselves for a big game and entrepreneurs prepare themselves for important interviews. Authors are no different. They prepare themselves to write their next best-seller. Preparation helps you anticipate each part of your story and frees your creativity to develop entrancing ideas. Proper preparation will reduce any anxiety you have about your writing venture.

As an author, I believe that preparation is the most vital part of writing a book. I also believe that everybody has their own personal way of preparing. Writing is a creative activity in itself. I know several authors who each have their own unique preparation routines. It all depends on you and your personal preferences. In this chapter, I will discuss some of the best ways to prepare yourself for the task of writing, but it's up to you to pick out what suits you best.

So, exactly how *does* one prepare to write a great fiction novel?

The Meaning of Success

How does one define a writer? There are probably as many definitions as there are writers. Many would argue that a successful writer has a special talent or skill. Others would define a successful writer as one who has obtained special training or reached a certain level of notoriety. A writer may also be someone with connections in the publishing industry. Check out what some writers think in AmazonKDP's YouTube video, What Does It Take To Be a Writer.

Here is my personal definition: I believe a successful writer is a person with a talent for writing, who is also willing to devote time to perfecting their craft. The craft can be perfected through trial and error, by taking classes, or through self-education (by reading books like this one, for example). A successful writer is a person who can learn from the critiques of others and push himself to grow as a writer. A successful writer writes regularly, even when it's not relative to his or her current work. A successful writer writes and rewrites, edits and re-edits. A successful writer is passionate about getting across a message.

Of course, it helps to have connections in the publishing field. You can start building those relationships by attending writing events and seminars, all of which can help you improve your craft.

You may think a successful writer is one who ultimately gets published and makes enough money to retire at a young age. Although that level of success can be extremely difficult to achieve, it is not impossible. Most people know that J.K. Rowling, author of the Harry Potter series, started out as a struggling single mom. Today she is the well-known author of multiple books, many of which have since been turned into highly popular movies.

While connections in the writing world can definitely help you get ahead, it is essential to know what publishers and readers are looking for. There is nothing wrong with contacting publishers directly, to learn what they are interested in publishing. Check out bestseller lists and look for common subjects and themes. Monitor news outlets and keep abreast of trending topics of interest. All of these can help you frame your story as an audience magnet.

Maybe you are not interesting in being published. If you just want to write for yourself, you are still a writer; your definition of success is just narrowed down to an audience of one.

I highly recommend taking some time to write down your definition of success. Writing about it will help make it solid in your mind as you continue your literary quest.

Define Your Writing Goal

Once you have defined what it takes to be a successful writer, you should define your writing goal. If you've read any of my other books, then you know how much of an emphasis I place on setting goals, when it comes to being successful at anything. Setting goals as a writer is a little more complex than setting goals for dieting or fitness. Why? As a writer, you actually have *two* goals: your own personal goal and the goal of providing your audience with a satisfying experience.

Your personal writing goal is a variable. You might make it a long-term goal to write a novel or a short story or a series of stories. Your long-term goal could even be to become a published author. Your short-term goals should provide stepping-stones to your long-term goals and help you, slowly but surely, achieve ultimate success. For example, if you want to become a published author, then your short-term goal should include writing your first novel. However, to write your first novel, you will need an additional set of even shorter-term goals that include the completion of each chapter. To achieve those goals, you will probably need to set daily writing objectives. Many authors set a specific word count quota in order to help them stay on track and finish within a desired timeframe.

No matter what your writing goal may be, it is important to remember your ultimate objective. Every author must work toward this goal to be successful (by their definition). Part of that success means you must know how to gain popularity with your target audience; you must provide your readers with an **emotional experience.** To achieve this, you must first recognize why people want to pick up a book in the first place.

Most people who enjoy reading say they see it as an escape from their own reality. Many readers like to put themselves in a different world so that they can experience emotions they otherwise wouldn't encounter in everyday life. They like to feel moved, touched and inspired. They like to feel danger, fear, and suspense. They like to be moved to feel happiness and sadness.

This is why it is so important to learn multiple techniques and elements of fiction writing. If your book is boring and the pace drags, your readers will not be able to immerse themselves in the story and will more than likely put your book down after the first few pages. If your book is filled with conflict and emotion, your readers will get what they're looking for. You will learn more about how to successfully provide your readers with an emotional experience as we progress through this book but for now, take out a piece of paper, or your journal, and write down your two writing goals. For your fixed goal, you can simply state that you will provide your readers with an emotional experience. You can go back and make it more specific as you discover just what that takes.

Figure out What Writing Level You Are On

The next step is to figure out what level you are on as a writer. I say this because it helps you figure out where you currently are compared to where you want to be. When figuring out what level you are on, you must be completely honest with yourself, otherwise you will never advance. Writing levels generally begin with the novice and progress to the inexperienced writer, then the experienced writer, and culminate in the expert.

A **novice** writer is typically just starting out. That's okay – everybody has to start somewhere. A novice writer usually knows that he or she wants to write something and has the ambition to take them there, but may not understand what is necessary to really pack a punch with an audience or how to actually put a book together. An **inexperienced** writer is typically someone who has exercised their writing talent before and may know how to put a book together, but they still need to improve their skills and sharpen their craft. An **experienced** writer is dedicated to writing and probably attends classes, networking events, etc.; this writer may have even self-published a few times. An **expert** writer is one who has written several works, is familiar with the craft and the ins and outs of publishing, has connections among other writers and publishers, and may even have been published by a major publishing house.

Ask yourself where you think you stand on the writing spectrum and make a note of it. Part of your writing goal can be to move up a level until you've become an expert. Always remember that no matter what level you're on, there is always room for improvement; writing is a lifelong growth process.

Get Organized

As a writer, <u>organization</u> should be on the top of your priority list for two reasons. First, your workspace must be easy to navigate; you must know where to find things without wasting precious writing time hunting around. Secondly, people tend to work most efficiently and creatively in an uncluttered environment. A clean and neat working area can actually make you feel good about yourself, which only feeds productivity and creativity. I'm reminded of a friend who was visited in his office by a well-dressed and neatly coiffed woman. The lady took one look at his desk, piled high with papers and research books, sniffed slightly, and stated, "You know; a cluttered desk is a sign of a cluttered mind." My friend thought for a moment, looked up at the woman, and asked, "Then, what does an empty desk signify?"

Personally, I'm way too distracted by a mess; any type of clutter pulls my focus away from my work. Consequently, here are my personal workspace organizational tips:

- Keep a towel or duster nearby and dust your work area once a day. This helps keep your workspace clean and avoids upsetting your allergies, if you have any.

- Keep wires (such as your laptop charger, printer cord, and associated USB cables) together and organized, using twist ties.

- Put your pens, pencils, and scissors together in a pen holder; a spare coffee mug works great for this purpose.

- Keep your important papers together in a paper tray or a file rack.

- Avoid eating or drinking in your workspace, but if you do, clean up the area immediately afterwards.

Assuming that you're using a computer to write your book, it is also important to stay digitally organized. I know from personal experience that when you start to write a book on your computer, one document can quickly turn into many. I often use individual documents to track characters, chapter notes, a timeline of events, synopses, outlines, etc. It is easy to lose track of those files within your hard drive, especially if you have a lot of stuff on your system.

I have recently discovered that <u>Microsoft OneNote</u> can take care of all my digital organization concerns. This software acts as a digital notebook and allows you to keep all of your information in one place, yet order it in any number of different ways. If you have handwritten notes in a physical notebook, you can import them into the program, and in that way keep everything together and easily accessible. OneNote is available through Microsoft. If you're going to do a lot of writing, it's seriously worth downloading. OneNote has saved me a ton of time and energy!

If you aren't using a program like OneNote, my next best suggestion is to keep all your story resources in a single computer folder. For example, to organize your current writing project, you could create a folder on your desktop, name it after your story, and save everything in that single location. If your folder holds more than ten items, I suggest you organize them by creating subfolders within the master story folder. Order these folders according to what makes sense to you. You may wish to put all your preparatory information (your plot planning, character lists, etc.) in one folder, with your draft text in another. You may wish to keep each chapter's text and related research documentation in a separate folder. You may feel the need to organize your work in any number of ways. The key is to organize your work in a way that is fairly unambiguous and makes sense to you; after all, you want to be able to put your finger on any part of your project at a moment's notice.

Although you may not immediately identify these next items as aspects of writing, you do need to organize your time, your energy, and your money. If you are working under a deadline, you automatically understand the importance of managing your time. Even if you don't have an externally imposed deadline, I recommend setting a rough target date for completion of your next writing project, then scheduling your work to meet that objective.

Parkinson's Law states that work expands to fill the amount of time allotted to it. If you don't set a deadline, guess what? Your writing project may well take until doomsday to complete! You will work a lot more efficiently if you divide the work up into manageable chunks, then shoot to complete each chunk in a reasonable amount of time.

 Giving yourself a "due date" will stimulate you to write on a regular basis. Writing a book does take time, but if you manage it correctly, it's not as bad as it may seem. You can manage your time several ways, but the most popular time management technique for writing is to set a daily writing quota for yourself, in terms of number of words. There are two possible ways to set both a writing quota and a deadline. The first way is to decide how much you want to write each day and divide the total size of your book, in number of words, by the by that amount. This will give you the number of days it will take to complete your first draft. You can map this on a calendar to determine your projected completion date. The other method is to decide when you want to finish your first draft, then work backwards from that date, calculating how many writing days you have before the deadline. Divide the total estimate for the book's word count by the number of days you plan to work, and you will know how many words you will need to write each day in order to meet your deadline.

Managing your time also includes planning breaks. Our bodies were not designed to sit still for hours on end. Recent studies have shown that as little as three hours of inactivity can be enough to affect our bodies negatively. Eyestrain is also possible in this line of work. It is important to take the eyes off the computer at least a couple times an hour, to look around you. When you can, take a few minutes outside; your eyes need to relax by looking into the distance for a change, and your whole being will benefit from a little intake of fresh air and natural sunlight.

We also need to periodically give our minds a break from thinking about the current writing project. Unfortunately, the mind does not have an "off" switch; the best way to give your mind a break is to divert it with something else that requires your attention. Any physical activity that requires a little attention will serve as a healthy break for both mind and body. I sometimes go outside to play with the dog or pull weeds in the garden. If I can't get outside, even a little light housecleaning is enough to get me moving and distracted from the computer for a few minutes.

The final organizational issue involves managing your money. You may not think about your writing costing any money and for the most part, you are correct. But you will likely incur a few expenses, if only for printer paper and ink for occasional printouts, and the cost of internet access, for conducting research and communication with potential publishers, etc. In addition, you may choose to invest in books that will help you as a writer; you may enroll in personal improvement classes, or pay for professional editing. Many writing seminars and conventions also cost money to attend. It is wise to allocate at least a small amount in your budget for writing expenses.

Pick a Writing Space

Every author needs a writing space – the place where you do the majority of your work. The most popular spots are at a desk in your home (preferably in a home office) or at a coffee shop, library, or another public venue. Some people can't focus when working in a public place like a coffee shop, but others thrive there. I've tried working on my laptop outside on several occasions but I've found it difficult when I don't have shelter from the sun. My personal preference is to sit at my desk and work. You might find comfort by working from your couch. Whatever you choose, set up your work in a comfortable location where you can work most productively.

Eliminate Distractions

As a writer, I must admit my top excuse for slacking off is any of the multiple distractions that come my way. Working on a computer can be the worst, because email, social media, music, and other attractive, activities are all too accessible. Even if you manage to avoid computer-based distractions, you can still access everything from your phone, which you probably keep close by. Then there are always the household distractions, your spouse, kids, or pets whose interruptions are almost irresistible. A quick and easy fix for this is to close the door to your office and hang up a do not disturb sign. I've tried writing outdoors before, but I've found that to be even more distracting than my children. I've endured everything from sunlight glaring on my screen, to babies crying in the neighborhood, to visits from stray dogs.

As for digital distractions, I've found it helpful to work in full-screen mode. This way, my eyes are less likely to wander off to whatever lies behind what I'm writing. I've also made it a point to mute my phone until I'm done writing. For audible distractions, I have discovered that earbuds will block out an incredible amount of noise, even without playing music through them.

Set the Mood

I personally find it helpful to set the mood before I begin a writing session. Depending on what kind of story I'm writing, I'll do different things. I've found that aromatherapy is a great strategy for relaxing and getting into a positive state of mind. You can practice aromatherapy right in your own workspace by getting a small oil diffuser and some different oils to experiment with. My favorite way to fill a room with pleasant smelling aromas is with an Aromatherapy Essential Oil Diffuser. I've never liked the heat based delivery systems of other products, but this diffuser releases a fine mist of sweet smelling aromas and turns off automatically when it is finished. Some great smelling essential oils I recommend are:

- Lavender – known for its relaxing qualities, it also smells heavenly.
- Eucalyptus – a strong earthy, but pleasantly scented plant, thought to clear the mind.
- Marjoram leaves
- Peppermint
- Chamomile
- Cloves
- Cinnamon Bark
- Sage,
- Rosemary,
- Cardamom
- Verbena

In other situations, I find it helpful to play music in the background while I'm writing. The type of music I listen to usually depends on the genre I'm writing, but I try to stick to instrumental tracks; tracks with lyrics tend to distract me. If I'm writing a sad or depressing scene I like to listen to classical music, such as Beethoven or Mendelssohn. If I'm writing a thrilling, action scene I'll go onto Spotify and look up soundtracks from my favorite movies to get me in the mood. If I can't really decide what to listen to, I'll just look up some Pandora instrumental tracks that are relaxing in general and let them play in the background.

Practice Self-Discipline

Writing a book will take lots of <u>self-discipline</u>. I've written and published several books and have had people come up to me and say, "Wow, I could never do that!" I can tell you that it's not easy and sometimes it is even tempting to give up. I've gone through phases where I will trudge right through a book and others where I'll start a book, only to drop it for a couple months. A disciplined life is essential if you hope to finish your book. For some people, self-discipline comes easily, but for those of you struggle to be disciplined, here are a few things you can do to reinforce your discipline choices:

1. Remind yourself of the consequences of *not* writing. A big self-discipline killer is when you say something along the lines of, "I'll do it when I feel like it." Well, what if you *don't* feel like it for the next couple of days? Let's say you have made it a goal to write one chapter of your book each day, but one morning you wake up and just don't feel like writing at all. Even a day or two without keeping your commitment to yourself will set you back to the point that it will be difficult to completely catch up. It is much better to meet your goals, even if it hurts. You will feel much better afterwards.

2. Stop making excuses. When it comes to writing a book, there are no excuses. Writer's block is not an excuse either. When you say something like, "I'm too tired to write today" or "I can't think of anything to write," you're only setting yourself back. Write something every day, even if it's just a little bit of free-writing. Never let an excuse take over your chosen life.

3. Get yourself an accountability partner. Find somebody who will hold you responsible for accomplishing the things you have committed to. This can be a huge help. My suggestion is to enlist the help of somebody who already serves as your mentor or role model; it will be harder to let down a person you respect and want to emulate than your best friend or your spouse. Sometimes best friends will let you off the hook far too easily. You want to find somebody who can be trusted to hold your feet to the fire when necessary.

Generate Self-Motivation

Along with self-discipline, you're going to need some <u>self-motivation</u> to get the job done. Procrastination is another obstacle that often prevents people from actually writing an entire book, so you'll need to know how to combat that before you even start.

One powerful technique that many authors use is to ask "why." Why do you want to write? Popular answers are so that you can see your name on the cover or so that you can entertain people. Some people simply have a story that they need to get out. Go ahead and figure out your why. I think it is helpful to write this down and keep it visible in your workspace, to consistently motivate yourself to keep going.

Another motivational technique is to promise yourself a reward at the end. Writing a book is a big task, so if you have a big reward waiting for you afterwards, you're going to be much more likely to finish. I can't tell you what your reward will be—that's up to you to choose—but make it something that you really, *really* want. You may choose a material object such as a new TV or video game system, others choose a short vacation, but for some people, just seeing the book in print is reward enough.

Finally, I have found that exercising can be motivational as well. Exercising allows your body to feel alive, so you'll have an overall "feel-good" sensation to carry into your writing. I think that the better you feel physically, the better you'll be able to perform your writing. When I work out, I start to feel inspired to tackle other major accomplishments. Exercising is also a useful way to spend your "break" time. You already spend enough time sedentarily before your computer; break it up by moving your body, and you may be pleasantly surprised with some fresh ideas when you return to your writing.

Eat Before Writing

One of the most important things you can do to get ready for writing is to eat beforehand! Eating a meal can give you a burst of mental energy, which you can then pour out into your book. If you try to write on an empty stomach, you may find it harder to concentrate; you might even do something crazy, like name a character after food! The best types of foods to eat before writing are those that will stimulate your brain. Here are a few examples:

1. Fruits and Vegetables – These foods are full of antioxidants that are good for fueling your creativity. Experts believe that blueberries are the most effective. Whip up some blueberry pancakes, a blueberry smoothie or simply just snack on some blueberries straight up.

2. Omega-3 Fatty Acids – This substance is known to boost the functioning of your brain, which you're definitely going to need as a writer. You can provide your body with omega-3 fatty acids through fish such as salmon or mackerel, or through flax seed. If you don't want to eat actual fish, you can always supplement your healthy diet with fish oil capsules.

3. Milk – Drinking milk can help boost your memory because it contains a wonderful substance called choline. As a writer, your memory is important; after all, you want the details in your story to be consistent. You don't want Mary to have blonde hair on page 3 and then brown hair on page 7.

4. Glucose – Foods that contain fructose can help your concentration remain solid. Avoid the high fructose corn syrup or alternative sweeteners. Stick to healthier natural sugars such agave and stevia, or eat some fresh fruit.

5. Protein and Whole Grains – Protein and whole grains are essentials for keeping your body energized and healthy. Your best bet is to eat a big breakfast that contains these nutrients. For example, try chowing down on some whole grain toast and an egg.

6. Supplements – In some cases you can take supplements to help boost your energy and mental clarity. Supplements come in all types, such as fish oil, multi-vitamins, individual vitamins, and minerals such as calcium with magnesium. One of my favorite supplements for mental activity like writing is called Focus Formula.

Find Your Niche Audience

Before you start writing, you'll have to figure out your niche audience. No book can ever appeal to everyone. Some books appear like they appeal to everyone, but that was not the case in the beginning. For example, people of all ages have read the Harry Potter series, but even those books originally started out as a series intended for school-age children. So yes, your book can eventually appeal to multiple audiences, but to become successful, it must first successfully reach a specific audience. It is important to remember that different people like different things. Not everybody within your niche audience is going to like your book, but as long as you can make much of your niche audience happy, then you will have succeeded.

The first step in figuring out your niche audience is to determine what types of people your book may interest. If you're writing a book about a love triangle, you would probably catch the interest of females. If you're writing a book about time travel, you'll likely interest people who are into science or history. Is your hero in the army? Then you might attract military veterans. Is your hero just starting out in high school? Then you'll probably attract teenagers. You get the picture.

Looking at demographics can also be helpful. The age of your main characters often will correlate with the age of your readers. Let's use Harry Potter as an example again. In the first book, Harry and his friends are about eleven years old and many kids who first read the book were around that age as well. As Harry and his friends grew up in the story, so did the readers.

Another powerful tool for determining your niche audience is to figure out what **emotions** you want to instill within your readers. Sometimes your readers will fall in love with your main character, either because they want to be him or they want to know somebody like him. An aspiring Marine might read a book about a Marine hero and a single mother might read a book about a heroic family man. You should also think about the emotions that the story itself invokes. Men tend to be more into action and adventure, so if your story contains those elements, your book will probably appeal more to men than to women. Women tend to enjoy romance and other chick lit, so if your book contains those elements, your audience will likely contain primarily women. Other genres tend to have a mixture of both male and female readers. Your audience depends on many factors, but having an idea of your book genre can definitely help you build your characters and their situations around themes that speak to your chosen target audience.

To get a good idea of how to define your niche audience, analyze your favorite books. By knowing what the story is about, can you figure out the intended audience for these books? The niche audience is not always who a book was originally written for; it is important to also look at who the audience ended up being. That will give you a great idea of *your* niche audience.

Once you have painted a picture of your audience, I recommend creating an **Ideal Reader Profile.** Businesses often do this, figuring out their target audience and creating an ideal customer profile. Having an Ideal Reader Profile on hand will enable you to easily identify potential readers. In this profile, write down any relevant details about your ideal reader, including religion, politics, education, gender, age, favorite reading genres, etc. This can also be helpful if you're planning to write multiple books for this audience. Some authors stick to a successful style and write books that appeal to the same niche audience.

Write a Book You'd Like to Read

Let's face it—people read books for entertainment and escape purposes, so a boring book won't really do any good. When you're preparing to write your book, plan to write something you would like to read. At least this will get you started on your way; it may even lead you to write a great novel! I recall once reading an interview with Lemony Snicker, the author of *A Series of Unfortunate Events*, in which he reported that his publisher asked him to write a book that he would have liked to read as a child. That's how his entire series came into being. Approaching your book from this perspective will also allow you to explore your creativity. Don't be afraid to mix different elements and ask "what if" questions to come up with crazy storylines. If you think it would be interesting, it probably will be. You will discover more on this element later on.

Settle on a Length

Before you actually start writing your book, one thing you should do is decide how long your book will be. The answer to this is that there *is* no "real answer." Your book can be as long as you want (or need). That being said, there are some common guidelines you can follow. If you plan on trying to get your book published, I strongly recommend calibrating your word count with these genre guidelines:

- Any type of adult novel – 80,000 to 100,000

- Chick lit – 70,000 to 75,000

- Sci-Fi/Fantasy – 110,000 to 115,000

- Young Adult – 55,000 to 70,000

- Children's – 20,000 to 55,000

- Picture books – 350 to 600

- Chapter books – 6,000 to 10,000

Here are also some general word count figures for these types of book:

- Short Story – 7,500

- Novelette – 7,500 to 17,500

- Novella – 17,500 to 40,000

Trying to write a book with a specific word count in mind can be challenging, especially if you're a first time writer. The real challenge lies in the fact that on one hand you don't want to compromise your story by leaving out critical details, but on the other hand, you don't want to overwhelm your story line with *too many* details. One great strategy is to decide what type of book you're going to write (so you have a rough idea of how long it should be), then write with no restrictions. See how many words you end up with and then edit them down as necessary. This way you have your entire book written so you can better decide what to edit out and which parts to keep.

Choose Your Emotional Drivers

Before you start writing your story, you need to decide what you want your readers to feel when they read it. These are your **emotional drivers**. To help you choose primary emotional drivers for your book, here is a brainstorming exercise:

Take out a piece of paper and start writing down a long list of emotions. Include any feelings you want. Once your list is complete, narrow down it down to two or three items. Select one primary emotion that is relevant to your genre. For example, a romance story would probably have love as its main emotion, whereas a memoir could have a main emotion of depression. The other emotions on your short list can be used to provide variety and depth to your main character.

Create an Outline

Some writers find it helpful to create an **outline** before writing. Others are better off just opening a blank document and typing away, making up the story as they go along. Personally, I am an outliner. I think about my story in depth and tend to put the story line together before I actually start crafting it, but that's just my preference. Outlining helps me ensure that my story flows, another quality that is immensely important to holding the attention of your audience. I also like to write a synopsis beforehand so I know exactly where each twist and turn fits into the overall shape of my story. If you are better off writing on a whim, you might consider writing an outline *after* you have written most of the book. Writing an outline after the fact will help you check for balance and continuity in your writing.

Terrible First Drafts and Painful Criticism

No great book was ever written in one sitting on the first try. One writer friend says he usually goes through seven drafts before he is satisfied about sending his book to the publisher. Don't worry about achieving perfection on your first draft. I'm a perfectionist myself, so I know just how challenging a first draft can be. However, I also know that writing a story is a complex task that will require multiple phases for its completion. The beauty of writing is that you can go back as many times as you want and edit your story until it really *is* perfect.

Now, pretend you've just finished the first draft of your novel and it feels great. You are certain you have the world's next best-seller lying on your desk. You send your "baby" to your editor or have somebody you trust critique your text; it comes back to you with all sorts of markings, indicating multiple suggestions for change. I know for a fact that this can be a serious blow to your ego. There's nothing more discouraging then to work hard at a creative task, only to have people find fault with it. However, remember this: yes, criticism hurts, but it's for the good of the book.

I remember the first story I published. I was so proud of it that I posted a couple chapters online to get readers' opinions. In retrospect, my first draft was absolutely terrible; I found out the hard way. After reading reams of solid criticism, I took another look at my tale and had to admit, "Actually, yeah this *is* pretty terrible." Only upon that admission was I able to go back and rework my story until I had come up with something worth releasing to the world.

Mentally prepare yourself for what feels like destructive feedback about your work. Remind yourself that critiques are *not* personal attacks; you requested the feedback in the first place. Secondly, those negative assessments of your work are not meant to destroy you, but to help you improve your book until it has become the best story you can make it.

Kickstart Your Creativity

In this final preparatory step, in order to start writing you will need to get your creativity going. Writer's block is often a writer's worst nightmare. There's nothing worse then getting everything ready, sitting down at your desk and then realizing that you don't know what you're doing. However, it is important to write *something* every day, whether or not it's relevant to your story. Your body, mind, and spirit need the repetition. I highly recommend that you sit down to write at about the same time every day; after you have done this consistently, your body and your mind will accept the activity as a habit, and you will suffer less mental resistance to writing than if your schedule were haphazard.

One of the most popular ways to meet this requirement as well as motivate yourself to work on your main story is **freewriting**. Freewriting is when you sit down and write whatever comes into your head. For freewriting to work best, you should set a limit, such as three minutes or three hundred words. This way you won't get lost in time, neither will you wear yourself out. Challenge yourself to write straight through without going back and making changes. If you really want to challenge yourself, close your eyes and don't look at what you've written until your time is up.

Another effective creativity strategy is to randomly pick a handful of letters from the alphabet and use those letters to create a potential title for a book. Then go ahead and start writing that story. Your tale can be as short or as long as you want. This strategy can serve as a warm-up to your writing project, or it could even turn into a full-length novel if you like the idea well enough.

If you're feeling really unmotivated, you could use a few "story starters" or writing assignments as a warm-up prompt. Creative Writing Now has some good writing prompts and story starters you can pick from to get started.

Sometimes when I'm feeling rather stale in the creativity department, I will take one of my favorite songs and make up my own lyrics. I'll usually make it about my friends or family and I'll work non-stop on it until I've written an entire parody song. That usually helps get my creativity flowing.

If you have already completed a book or a short story, a great creative writing strategy is to make up an alternative ending. Think about one of your favorite movies where they show another ending if you watch through the credits. If your story has a happy ending, maybe you could write up a more depressing ending. If your story has a sad ending, you can put a happy spin on it.

Alternatively, I sometimes find inspiration by reading one of my favorite authors' works, by watching a movie I've never seen before, or by playing a new role-playing game. I think that when I explore new experiences I am reminded that the creative possibilities out there are endless. This alone will often fire me up to get started writing again.

Chapter 2: Decisions, Decisions

Once you have accomplished the necessary preparation, the next step is to figure out the basics of your story. **Story basics** are things that you need to ask yourself, such as "What type of book will this be?", "Where is the story set?", or "Where will the story begin?" Once you have these details worked out then you can delve into the actual writing. In this chapter, you will discover how to strategically set up your book to be a best-seller by selecting your genre, setting, action and other foundational items.

What is a Story?

A story forms when characters want what that they can't have; usually, this will involve them in some sort of **change**. Readers generally like to see your main character change and grow across the life of the story. The change should be realistic, because your readers will be experiencing it through the eyes of your main character. , when a character sees something in their life differently, views the world differently, or learns something about themselves near a genuine change will occur near the end of your story. As your main character experiences growing discomfort–or a cataclysmic event–he is often pushed into an internal confrontation, which generates **conflict**. Alternatively, the conflict may occur first, driving your character toward internal change. As the main character undergoes change, this process will help shape your **plot.**

Why Write This Story?

Is your story intended to educate your readers? Are you writing purely to entertain? Are you trying to persuade them? Many stories within the categories of historical or military fiction are almost automatically educational. Other educational novels provide an inside look at human nature. Stories based on social issues are easily persuasive in nature. No matter your purpose, the most important thing to determine next is what genre is most effective for your story.

Pick Your Genre

Genre is somewhat important to publishers and, ultimately, to your readers. It enables both to quickly identify your book describe your book to others and list it appropriately online when you do get it published. It's easier to tell people, "It's a romance thriller," than to explain, "It's a book about a guy and a girl who meet and fall in love, but there are conflicts and plot twists before they decide what to do." Here are some most common literary genres:

- Romance – a story in which sparks fly between two characters who work toward living "happily ever after." Subgenres of romance may include erotica, lgbtq (lesbian, gay, bisexual, transgendered, questioning), paranormal, new adult, comedy, suspense, science fiction or fantasy.

- Thriller/Suspense – When something bad is about to happen to the main character and she attempts to escape harm's way. Subgenres include crime, historical, legal, medical, military, political, psychological, and techno.

- Mystery – A story that focuses on solving a crime or uncovering a secret. Subgenres of mystery include historical, international, and women's mysteries.

- Science Fiction – A story based in some aspect of science, often set in the future or on another planet. Subgenres of science fiction include adventure, aliens, cyberpunk, high-tech, post-apocalyptic, space operas, steampunk and time travel.

- Fantasy – A story that focuses on mystical or foreign creatures, often creating its own from. Subgenres of fantasy include dark, epic, magical realism, myths and legends, paranormal, and superheroes.

- Horror – A story that focuses on scaring the reader. Subgenres of horror include ghosts, monsters, gore, zombies, witches, and the supernatural.

- Historical Fiction – A fictional story set in an historical era. Subgenres of historical fiction include African American, biographical, Christian, cultural heritage, Jewish, mysteries, thrillers, and fantasy.

- Women's Fiction – Fiction marketed to women, containing women's issues and often written by women. Subgenres of women's fiction include African American, contemporary women, domestic life, mothers, children, and sisters or friends.

- Children's Fiction – Stories geared toward children, ranging from toddlers to about twelve years of age.

- Young Adult – A story written for audiences ranging from twelve to eighteen years old. The main character is often the same age as the reader. Subgenres of young adult include mysteries, thrillers, sports, social issues, biographies and general fiction.

- General Fiction – A story written purely from the imagination and made-up; not based on factual persons or events. This may also refer to a book that does not fit neatly into any of the other categories; it could be an equal mixture of two or more genres.

Some less popular genres include erotica, metafiction, philosophical fiction, religious fiction, dystopian fiction, supernatural, paranormal, and westerns.

Choose your Setting

The **setting** of your book is important to choose early on, because it will serve as the world in which your story plays out. One of the best things about a setting is that it can range from plain and simple, to highly complex. Warning: It is easy to get so caught up in developing your plot or your characters that you fail to create the world they inhabit. On the other hand, by selecting a specific setting you create a framework which can actually help you define both your characters and the plot. Here are some points to consider when choosing your setting:

Universe/World – Will your story take place right here on Planet Earth, or will it be set in another realm? Good examples of books that have used creative settings are the *Lord of the Rings* series, *Alice in Wonderland*, the *Harry Potter* series, and *The Wizard of Oz*.

You can set your story anywhere you want, and you can make the setting as broad or as localized as you choose. You can place it nearby or in a foreign culture, in a big city, a small town, on a beach, or even in the middle of an ocean. Think about whether you want to set your tale in a country, in a region of the country, or in a specific city in that country. Would you rather restrict the setting to a small town or a specific neighborhood? Your setting can be as specific as a certain street, house, or building. It can also range as widely as the universe

Time and Date – Setting a clear era for your book to inhabit is important in helping your readers visualize the story. Some authors choose to draw out a timeline in their books, but that step is optional. However, it is important to state or at least hint at the age in which your book is set so that readers have an idea of how your characters will dress, act, and talk. Once you have set your timeframe, you will need to check periodically for time discrepancies. For example, if your book is set in the 1950s, your characters cannot just whip out their cell phones and exchange phone numbers. Especially when I am writing historical fiction, I like to use actual dates in my chapter names, to give my readers a feel for the passage of time.

It is sometimes of key importance to tell or imply what time of day a scene takes place. I would, however, avoid an opening line like Snoopy's, "It was a dark and stormy night." Surely you can utilize your descriptive skills to *show* what's going on rather than overtly *tell* it. Here is an good example of implying a setting: "Johnny slid in the fresh dew that lingered on his front lawn." The start of a chapter or a section is a good place to clue in your readers regarding how much time has elapsed since the previous section. Once again, use your descriptive skills to weave implications into your text.

Atmosphere – Describing the atmosphere of your setting helps to set the moods within your story. You can use the weather or the lighting or some other external factor to set the mood, but do so sparingly. I've heard that publishers are turned off by stories that start by describing the weather. Once again, as with showing the time of day, work the atmosphere into your story by describing it rather than *telling* the details. For example, if the atmosphere is intended to be dark and sinister, instead of saying, "It was really dark and ghosts screamed in the background", you could more tactfully say your main character "peers uneasily into the pitch dark night, all the more nervous because he is unable to see the source of the evil laughter that seems to surround him."

Geography – The geography of your setting can help frame the action in your story. Geography includes climate, plant life, bodies of water, and other land masses. Perhaps your main character goes to the beach every day until she meets her true love. Or, maybe your story is a fairy tale set in the middle of the woods, where the main characters chop down trees for firewood. I didn't think geography mattered at first, but it really does. Your characters that live near the beach probably have a very different lifestyle from the mountain dwellers.

Historical Context – If your story revolves around an important historical event, such as a war or a tsunami, include that event in your setting. This will anchor the story in time for your readers; it also helps fit your book into the historical fiction genre, if this is your objective.

Politics, Economics, Sociology, Religion – These factors play into your setting and can dramatically affect the behaviors and the personality of your characters. A character who lives in the projects will act differently from one who lives in an affluent neighborhood. Likewise, a character who is a practicing Catholic could well have different reactions from one who is an agnostic. Considering these factors can also help you with set up the conflict. You have a built-in conflict brewing if your character is raised in a high-status background, but finds himself living in a slum. Alternatively, your agnostic character who finds herself forced to attend a Catholic school will be in for an experience she can either embrace or reject. Brainstorm some ideas surrounding these contexts and see what conflicts or plot twists you can come up with.

Your book's physical setting can be complex, affecting even minor details, such as mannerisms, food or language. Setting can also be effective when it is kept to a few stark specifics. You can use subtle or lavish amounts of imagination, although I personally prefer the risk of erring in excess.

Research your world thoroughly, if you're not creating it from scratch. For example, if you plan to set your story in New York City, I highly recommend spending at least a day there to get a feel for what goes on, in addition to looking it up in newspaper articles and YouTube videos. Even if you are from New York and know every borough intimately, I suggest you take a day to play tourist, giving yourself a chance to view the old and familiar through fresh eyes.

What Makes Your Story Interesting?

One of your goals as a writer should be to write a story that will stand out and grab the interest of your readers. Picture them picking up your book and just dying to turn each page to find out what happens next. However, for that to happen, your book must be interesting, with fully fleshed out characters and a well-rounded story arc.

First, you should consider the plot. What is your plot? What kind of plot twists do you want to use? A good plot contains **exposition** (background descriptions to set the story and introduce the plot), **rising action** (the events, conflicts, twists and turns that lead to the high point of the story), a **climax** (the high point, where conflict elements really hit the fan), **falling action** (resolution of ongoing conflicts, filling in gaps that would otherwise leave your audience hanging in suspense) and a **resolution** (bringing the story to a satisfying end).

Additionally, your story should have an early **hook**, something to swiftly engage your reader and make them want to read more. I've been advised to open my stories with some sort of disturbance, because a well-written disturbance automatically piques reader curiosity and raises questions about the back-story, the characters, and their motives. Your hook can be as intense as two people exchanging gunfire, but it may also appear in more subtle form, such as a distressed mother trying to calm a crying baby. One way to determine if your story has a good hook is to see if it leaves readers wanting to know what happens next. For example, a book that opens up with a crying baby would probably make readers ask, "What is causing the baby to cry and how will the mother, who is seemingly stressed out and under pressure, react?"

Create a Plot Twist

A **plot twist** is essential to sustaining reader interest. You want to ensure that your story is not boring. At the same time, you don't want to introduce a plot twist so crazy that it's completely unbelievable. So, how do you go about creating a good plot twist? When one friend was writing her first novel, she was stumped for the longest time about how to make her story intriguing. Then one day, as she was taking a walk, a plot twist just popped into her mind out of nowhere. Some writers get lucky that way, but if your plot twist doesn't come to you like a gift, I have a few exercises that may help stimulate some ideas.

One powerful exercise is to brainstorm a list of possible—and impossible—plot twists. Write at least ten ideas if not more. Consider each idea, no matter how implausible, because even crazy ideas can sometime spawn brilliant ones.

Another suggestion is to read your story, looking for any scenes that might contain potential clues to a plot twist. For example, my friend originally wrote a scene in which her two main characters, a pair of former lovers, met up on a street corner, after having no contact for over three years. During their conversation, the female character mentioned she had some news to share. However, before she had a chance to let it out, the two got into an argument and the woman left without revealing her secret. That scene contained plenty of wiggle room for the author to experiment with until she could figure out how to use the untold secret as the setup for a major plot twist.

It helps to develop two or three plot twists that lead into each other. An easy way to do this is to follow a basic **three act structure** for your book. In this structure, your story will have a beginning, a middle, and an end. Set your hook and create tension in the beginning of the story with the first twist, using any type of challenge, obstacle or disturbance. In this section, make extensive use of exposition and dialogue to introduce your readers to the setting and the main characters.

In the middle of your story, insert another twist. Make this plot twist a little more dramatic than the first one. Let this plot twist serve as the "point of no return" for your main character. Once he or she encounters this twist, there is nowhere to go but ahead. Make this plot twist life-changing. This part, the middle of your book, should take up the majority of your content.

Toward the end of the middle section, insert your third plot twist, which will lead directly to the climax, the beginning of the end. This challenge or obstacle should ultimately lead to the resolution of all the individual threads in your story. In the climax, your protagonist will often be called on to make some sort of decision. In many stories, this twist will set up the final confrontation, either between two characters or within the main character. You must clearly show whether or not your main character has accomplished the goal set out earlier in the book. You may choose any type of ending. Although many readers look forward to a happy ending, sometimes your story will call for one that is sad or bittersweet.

Inference

Narrative summary, a simple recitation of actions and the explicit statement of emotions or motives, makes for a boring, flat novel. If you leave nothing unsaid, you will be cheating your reader's imagination. That is why I keep saying **show, don't tell**. Let your readers exist inside the story, viewing their surroundings as they view real life. In real life, nobody is handed all the information; most of the time, we have to infer motives and emotions by observing the circumstances in our larger environment. For example, take a look at the two passages below and ask yourself which one sounds better:

Passage A – John got into the car after hotwiring it under the hood. The cops were starting to catch up with him. John wasn't sure if he was going to make it out alive. The cops were getting closer and closer. All he cared about was getting away so that he could see his daughter again.

Passage B – The car door slammed behind John as he threw himself into the driver's seat of the silver sports car. His ears were still ringing from the blaring car alarm. Sweat poured down his forehead as he nervously looked over his shoulder for any witnesses. A knot suddenly balled up in his stomach as he saw the flashing lights of red, white and blue in the distance behind him. Just as his ears settled, they began to ring with the faint sound of sirens, gradually getting louder and louder. Before putting the car into drive and slamming his foot down on the gas pedal, he grabbed his wallet and flipped it open to a picture of a young girl – his daughter – and said to himself, "This one's for you."

Both passages made available the basic facts. However, the second paragraph sounds a lot better, right? You can actually feel the nervousness and tension of the main character through the description of his physical experience. As you read about the sweat dripping, ears ringing, and the knot in his stomach, you actually start to feel the tension along with the character. You have successfully tricked your mind into a state similar to the character's.

I'll bet the second paragraph also held your interest a lot better than the first one. Readers don't want to read something that is long, boring and dragged out. Think of it this way: If you were a college student, would you select a class under a professor who stands in front of the class and speaks in a monotone, or would you prefer one who moves around and puts some zest into his lecture?

Notice how the second paragraph employs multiple senses in its description of the action. Touch, taste, sight, sound, and smell are powerful senses in real life; they can be just as useful when writing a story. Take note of how I used the senses if sight and sound to enhance the second paragraph. If you were to use taste, you could take a flat sentence such as "the chocolate cake with vanilla icing tasted good" and turn it into "Warm, gooey chocolate dripped out of the freshly baked cake as it sat on the platter, waiting to be topped off with sweet vanilla icing." Which sentence makes your mouth drool?

Mechanics are Important

Use correct spelling, Standard English grammar, and appropriate punctuation in your story. Exceptions are only allowed when slang phrases suit your environment or when you have a character who speaks with an accent. There's nothing more annoying than trying to read a book with multiple errors; every mistake is a slap in the face of a reader. Always pay a proofreader to take a last look at your work before sending it off; you need a fresh set of eyes to see what you can't and the small price is well worth paying for the peace of mind you gain.

If you plan to publish your tale as an eBook, take the time to ensure that your book is formatted correctly for all platforms. Again, there's nothing worse than downloading a book and not being able to read it smoothly on your screen. Improper formatting only makes your text harder to follow; you also run the risk of your readers requesting a refund and leaving a bad review in their wake.

Chapter 3: She's Quite a Character

Carefully developed characters are probably the most important element to crafting an interesting story. Characters are the heartbeat of your book; they drive your plot forward and, when your readers fully identify with a character, it helps them fully immerse in the story. Since they are so important, you'll need to know how to create fully-developed, dynamic characters for your story. This chapter will show you how.

Choose Your Major Characters

How many characters belong in one story? There really is no concrete answer. At minimum, you'll need at least one character, your main character, who can be a protagonist, antagonist or antihero. Most novels have at least one protagonist and one antagonist. If you only have one character, then his or her opponent in conflict will likely be the inner self, although some survival stories feature natural phenomena as the antagonist.

Protagonist

A protagonist is the main character of your book, also known as a central character, major character, a dynamic or a round character. This main character must be one with whom your readers can identify. A protagonist is never perfect; in fact, your character's flaws are often what create the story's conflict. You will probably put a lot of effort into creating and understanding your protagonist. He or she must be as true-to-life as possible; after all, this is who your readers will follow throughout the entire story. Let your central character develop and grow across the span of your story. Readers like to watch a protagonist undergo substantial change; this is what they experience in their lives. Keep in mind that your readers are often drawn to a book because they are hungry to learn how another person solved a problem that is similar to their own.

I find that making your protagonist as true to life and as detailed as possible can help bring him or her to life. I do this by answering as many questions as possible about my protagonist. For example, I ask myself:

- Where does my character live? With whom does he live?

- What type of dwelling does he live in? How did he come to live there? Does he like it?

- Where is he originally from? What is his background?

- How old is my protagonist? (This is a very important question, because it determines so many other details).

- What is my protagonist's name? How does this reflect his personality, his background, and even possibly, the challenge he will face in this book?

- What is the social class of my protagonist?

- What does my protagonist look like? (The more detailed a description, the better).

- What was his childhood like and how does it affect him now?

- What does my protagonist do for work? Does he work at all?

- How does my protagonist handle change/conflict?

- What kind of relationships does he have?

- What is his goal?

Let these questions branch off into sub-questions. For example, when you ask yourself about your protagonist's childhood, explore whether he was raised by a single mother, by an abusive father, or by adoptive parents. By answering these questions, you are creating a solid framework for your book. For example, if you decide that your protagonist is a sixteen-year-old boy, you wouldn't write a scene with him drinking in a bar unless you're painting him as a defiant teen. Avoid letting your protagonist live an unchanging and boring life; otherwise you will not hold your readers' attention long enough to reach the checkout lane.

Describe Your Protagonist Early

It is crucial for your readers to get acquainted with your protagonist early in the story; otherwise, they will be less likely to identify places where inner growth and change may occur. Think of your story's beginning as a snapshot of your protagonist in his or her "lost" state. Ensure that your readers understand who your protagonist is at the beginning, so they will better comprehend the changes, challenges, sacrifices and obstacles he will go through en route to becoming a more "complete" person. For example, let's review the storyline from the movie *Shrek*. In the beginning, Shrek was a miserable, lonely monster who had no friends and projected a generally negative attitude. However, by the end of the story, the events, challenges, and friendships he experienced had changed him into a happily married, positive-thinking monster. The ending wouldn't have been significant at all if Shrek had remained unchanged.

Here are some additional questions to focus on once you've settled on the basics of your protagonist:

- What goes on around your protagonist and what goes on inside his head as a result? In other words, which external factors act as a stimulus for which internal factors? If your protagonist is a generally moral person but he loses his home and is forced to live under a bridge, where might that lead? The conflict between external circumstance and internal morals will be the drawing factor of your book. Your protagonist is faced with a choice: will he violate his morals by breaking the law to survive, something he would have never done earlier, or will he discover another way out of his dilemma?

- What will be the trigger that moves your protagonist to change? Perhaps she is required to overcome a specific character weakness in order to achieve "completeness." Another main character may suddenly, in an "aha" moment, discover he now knows what is happening or he now has what he needs to emerge from his difficulty. This sudden knowledge will often trigger your final plot twist and lead directly to the climax of your story.

- Why is it significant for your protagonist to reach "completeness?" To answer this question, think in terms of life lessons. Readers like to feel your story has a message; in many cases this theme will come in the form of a moral or a life lesson that becomes apparent by the end of the story. For example, the life lesson in *Hansel and Gretel* is to never take candy from strangers. The two protagonists are completely unaware of this advice until they've survived a terrible experience as a result of taking candy from a stranger. Odds are, if a sequel to that fairy tale was ever written, Hansel and Gretel would probably display a healthy distrust toward strangers bearing candy.

- What has to happen by the end of the story in order to make your protagonist "complete?" The answer to this question is often a high-stakes climax followed by an engaging victory. Think of it as "the final standoff" or a life-changing event that firmly establishes the resolution. For example, in *The Wizard of Oz*, Dorothy finally gets her chance to go home. However, she fails to make it into the balloon with the wizard, so poor Dorothy–along with the waiting public–thinks she's stuck in Oz forever. When she clicks her heels three times and wakes up in her own bed, Dorothy realizes how grateful she is for her family, because she thought she had lost them forever. Because of the double scare, Dorothy will never again resent her "boring" existence.

- Does your protagonist gain redemption in the end? Will he be required to sacrifice something to reach his goal? Hero figures often make a major sacrifice before they can succeed. In a traditional hero story, the hero often sacrifices his or her life for the good of the people, but it doesn't have to play out that way. In the first *Spiderman* movie, Peter Parker sacrifices his chance for a relationship with M.J., in order to protect his identity and continue to protect the people. Readers like to see a protagonist make a sacrifice, because it is inspiring. Your character gives up something he values in order to benefit somebody else.

Alternatively, your protagonist may be an **Anti-Hero**. An anti-hero protagonist does not have the traditional positive qualities of a regular protagonist and is often immoral, self-centered, or unheroic. Some anti-heroes have addictions or are involved in some sort of corruption. However, an anti-hero usually grows into a more complete person by the end of the story, even though that growth often comes at the cost of his life. Anti-heroes often inspire readers to overcome their own insecurities.

A Well-rounded Protagonist

Good protagonists should contain enough detail of character to make them interesting individuals. Here are some points to consider:

First of all, your protagonist needs a **personality**; otherwise you're drawing with a white crayon on white paper, so to speak. You want your protagonist to jump off the page and into the hearts of your readers. The best way to create a strong personality is to answer as many questions as you can about his background. You'll want to be able to explain and predict your protagonist's thoughts and feelings.

Exercises

You can increase your personality develement skills by participating in method acting classes or stream of consciousness exercises. The activity below may also be of help:

I'm a big fan of voice recorders; I think talking into a voice recorder as if you were your protagonist can be a very helpful creative exercise. To experience this exercise, begin by introducing yourself and then speak as if you were that character and see what comes out. Try this for at least ten minutes, since you will need a little time to get used to the concept and really get into your character. Your brain could very well start making up things you think are genius. When you are finished, replay the tape to glean the best parts for your protagonist.

A good way to add some personality to your protagonist is to **exploit her fear**. Just because your protagonist isn't real doesn't mean she can't feel fear. We all have fears; just connect your protagonist's fears to the story line. This will help your character seem more real and believable. A fearless protagonist (unless it makes sense in the story) will all too often come across as robotic and nonhuman.

You also need to decide what your protagonist's **internal conflict** will be. Internal conflict is when your character wants two things but is unsure which one to pick or how to get both. The best way to capture your readers' attention and take them on a psychological joyride is to create an internal conflict that is emotional and testing. Try to stay near to a type of internal conflict you might find in yourself one day.

Once you've figured out the internal conflict, you'll also want to determine the **external conflict.** External conflict is driven by an outside factor that is somehow related to the internal conflict. For example, in the internal conflict, your protagonist has to pick between fleeing his hometown and remaining in an unhealthy and unsafe environment. If you add in an assassin who is chasing your protagonist, that will serve as your external conflict.

Next, your protagonist needs **motivation.** A character's motivation is usually connected to her values and ambitions as well as her goals. A good way to portray motivation in your story is to give your protagonist two clashing values, which will create internal conflict; then your character will be forced to pick between them. Ambition, which represents what your protagonist wants more than anything, will be the driving motivation. Limit your protagonist's ambition to one thing. Her ambition will move her to choose between options and can be the driving force behind her actions.

Your protagonist should also have **relationships** with other characters in your story. Most often, your protagonist will have an existing relationship with the antagonist, as well as with minor characters; all relationships can help push your story forward. A lone ranger protagonist can easily dry up very quickly, unless he has other people in his life. Relationships make it possible for your protagonist to connect with your readers. Your audience wants to identify with the main character; that's one of the main reasons he or she is reading your book. For example, young adult books are specifically written for young adults, with characters of the same age who experience similar conflicts to the typical young adult.

Give your protagonist a unique **voice.** This often includes the way your character speaks and moves. For example, if your protagonist is a gangster, he might talk using jargon specific to gangsters and he may stalk rather than walk. If your protagonist is a professor of physiology, she would probably speak with advanced vocabulary and complex sentence structures. Giving your protagonist a unique voice helps establish your main character's personality. It can even reflect part of a backstory. For example, if your character stutters, his voice could link to a past that involved bullying or abuse.

Similarly, your protagonist should be full of **emotion.** An emotionless protagonist is worse than watching paint dry. For example, if your protagonist is in the middle of a break-up with someone else, think about what emotions will come into play. Often the other person will be extremely upset and will cry, beg, or otherwise try to convince your protagonist not to walk away. All the while, the main character is resistant to these emotions and just wants out of the relationship once and for all. In another scenario, think about all of the emotions present in a wedding scene. The feelings would be mostly positive, but think about an a parent's objection or something else that could go wrong. Examine many possible scenarios and use their related emotions to your advantage when you write.

Give your protagonist at least one **strength** and one **flaw.** A protagonist with no strengths at all is pretty boring and one-dimensional. So is one with no flaws. What's the point of reading about your protagonist if he or she doesn't have anything human to offer or any space for growth? If you give your protagonist an amazing strength, also include a character flaw. the juxtaposition of these two character traits opens up all sorts of possibilities to generate conflict. For example, your character in a love story could be a genius in the computer lab, but at the same time be horribly clumsy when it comes to dating.

What else makes for a good protagonist? One key is inclusion of a **mystery** or a **secret.** This works best if one character is already mysterious and another one has a secret; the secret may explain why the other character is so mysterious. For example, let's say you are writing a story about a love triangle, in which your protagonist skips town with the woman of his dreams but still stays in touch with his ex. The ex has a secret; she is carrying his child, or she has some sort of incurable disease. The new girlfriend doesn't know this secret, so her boyfriend's mystique drives her crazy. If your readers don't know the secret either, they will be driven crazy as well and are all the more likely to read to the end of your book in their quest to uncover the secret.

The majority of readers like to see a protagonist with lots of courage, inner strength, sex appeal, mental sharpness, generosity, kindness, or selflessness. However, fiction is fiction, so it's totally up to you and your story, what kind of person you want your protagonist to be. Of course, if your protagonist is an anti-hero, you won't make him selfless or genuinely caring.

One of the best things about fiction is that following these rules is somewhat optional. I say "somewhat" because you must know the rules thoroughly before you can understand when you can get away with bending, or outright breaking them. Nine times out of ten, it is best to stick closely to the rules if you want to be successful, but you know what they say about rules being built to be broken. There's really no straight answer. You could play by the rules and write a flop; you could also deviate from them and discover you've captured your audience with a completely new concept.

While we have focused on developing a powerful protagonist you can apply all of these tools to your other characters; for a successful book, you need a well-rounded cast. If your protagonist is fully developed but is surrounded by flat, one-dimensional characters, you'll still have a weak storyline.

Antagonist

The antagonist is a character in your story who goes up against the protagonist. He or she usually stirs up conflict, sometimes just by entering the scene. In some stories the antagonist is very clear, but in others it's not as easy to pick out. Think of the antagonist as the personification of an obstacle your protagonist must overcome. Sometimes the antagonist is referred to as the **foil**, which describes a contrasting character, in terms of personal qualities.

Minor Characters

These are characters who assist in moving the story forward or serve as a contrasting personality. They can provide depth to more important characters by opening up backstory elements. **Stock Characters** are flat, stereotypical individuals who are easily identified, such as the mad scientist or the nerd. However, use stock characters sparingly. A story peopled by stock characters can seem cartoonish and is difficult to elevate beyond boring.

One Main Question, One Main Goal

As I mentioned earlier, your story should have a single main question, which usually connects with the goal of your protagonist. For example, Indiana Jones usually goes off looking for treasure, which provokes the readers to ask, "Will he find the treasure?" Your story may generate multiple questions, but one should always be primary.

To ensure that your round characters stay round, every character should have a goal. The most important goals are usually the conflicting objectives that strike sparks between your protagonist and antagonist. For example, Spiderman (the protagonist) wants to protect the city while the Green Goblin (the antagonist) wants to destroy him—and it. Spiderman also wants M. J. (a minor character) to fall in love with him, while she is more focused on becoming an actress. People who watch the movie find themselves asking questions about both unknowns. Notice how all three of these characters have goals that help move the story forward.

Keep a Character List

I highly recommend creating and keeping a character list to prevent and eliminate inconsistencies. For example, if you write in the beginning that your character has brown eyes you don't want to describe her eyes as blue a few chapters later. A detailed character list that includes physical characteristics, mental traits and the personal background will remind you at a glance that your character has brown eyes. My artistic capability scarcely extends beyond stick figures, but if you can draw, I highly recommend setting down a highly detailed visual representation of your characters, especial the primaries.

Backstory

Alright, let's talk more about the backstory. Backstories can serve as a useful tool to flesh out your various personalities. A character's backstory is what helps your readers understand where he is coming from–quite literally, what causes her to drop to the ground whenever lightening explodes, or why he carries that enormous chip on his shoulder. It is essentially the history of your character. Although your protagonist's backstory is often the most important, all your characters can become more realistic if hints to their backstories are dropped periodically.

One mistake I have made–and had to repent from–is to focus so strongly on a character's backstory that I fail to pay enough attention to the development of the plot. The strongest character in the world cannot overcome a lame plot.

Also, don't make the mistake of turning your first few chapters into a backstory. A backstory is just that, an entirely separate story. Call it a prequel if you will, but only publish it *after* your current novel has become successful!

Flashbacks are a useful tool to reveal aspects of a character's backstory. I know one author who has utilized flashbacks to complement what she was actually writing and it worked out well. What she did was to start telling the main story about a girl who was kidnapped, then she sprinkled snippets of backstory throughout the book in the form of flashbacks. As you read through the book, you learn what the girl had been doing prior to being snatched, and you also discover why her abductors were so crazy as to nab her. flashbacks not only help round out the characters, they also keeps the readers' curiosity piqued for new information.

If you're going to use flashbacks to tell your story, be careful to transition smoothly back and forth between them and your story's present tense. One straightforward method is to start a flashback as a new scene, indicating it by using the simple past tense. When you end the flashback, close out the scene and switch back to the present tense, continuing the main story.

The great thing about a backstory is that you can create it up front or develop it as you go along. I find that having a general idea of a character's backstory is good enough for starters. You can flesh out the details as you write. Having a backstory all written out in front of you helps you keep track of your story's context. This is especially useful if you have an extensive backstory for multiple characters.

I recommend using backstory development as a warm-up for additional writing. Just select a character and start developing a backstory. Don't worry; your backstory can evolve as your story develops. Then, as you write your main book, you can decide what snippets or details from the backstory will help move your story forward.

Interior Monologue

Knowing how to use interior monologue (essentially getting into the head of your character) is useful is highly useful. There are two types of interior monologue – direct and indirect. Direct interior monologue is when your character is speaking directly from inside her head. Many authors use italics to indicate this. Here is an example of direct interior monologue:

"The only thing that could complete her day trip was if she had someone with her besides her boring parents. Anyone, really. A cousin, a friend…a boyfriend. *Like I'll ever have one of those.*"

Direct interior monologue is also best written in first person present tense, as you can see in the example above. Putting direct thoughts in italics helps them stand out to the reader. That being said, you should try to use italicized direct interior monologue sparingly, otherwise it will lose its special flavor.

Indirect interior monologue exists when the author tells you a character's inner thoughts as narrative description. Here is an example:

"Being home schooled was something that Emily didn't like to share. It embarrassed her to talk about it."

Sometimes, a tag, such as "he said" or "she thought" is necessary to keep straight who is thinking what. For example:

"*I have been angry ever since school started*, he thought to himself."

Most authors I know use a mixture of direct and indirect interior monologue to reveal their characters' internal processing. People sometimes read fiction because the interior monologue enables them to see what a character is thinking, as opposed to guessing from the action, as in a movie.

Interior emotions can help develop your character. Interior emotion tells readers about your character by showing their emotions. For example, if your character is scared, you can describe the physical effects of fear such as starting to sweat, or a racing heart. Don't come right out and say that he's scared. That's narrative summary, something I already warned you to avoid for the most part. If you are unsure how to work interior emotion into your scene, just ask yourself, "What is my character feeling and what does that look like?" Similes and metaphors can add power to your descriptions of interior emotion. Just use highly clichéd examples very sparingly.

Developing Character Through Dialogue

Dialogue is one of the most important factors in fiction because it helps develop your characters and push your plot forward. That being said, the dialogue in your book must be perfectly crafted. Alfred Hitchcock once said that a good story is "life with the dull parts taken out." In other words, readers don't want to read something like this:

"What do you want for lunch today? PB and J?"
"Oh yeah, that sounds good."
"Okay, I'll go make you one right now."

Boring, right? Dialogue requires focus, impact and relevance to be effective. It needs to push your plot forward or reveal something about your characters. For example, let's rewrite the above example to create some conflict and introduce tension between the characters:

"What do you want for lunch today? PB and J?"
"All you ever feed me is PB and J. You never let me pick what *I* want to eat."
"If you're going to be so picky about the food we eat, maybe you should get a job sp you can buy your own food."

Dialogue Tips

I personally believe that writing good dialogue stems out of the "practice makes perfect" philosophy. The more you experiment with it, the more naturally your dialogue will sound. Nonetheless, here are some things to keep in mind when writing dialogue:

1. Don't give out too much information at once. Let tidbits slip out in normal conversation. If you try to force information on your reader, your characters may sound stilted and you may find yourself overusing narrative summary. Instead, keep your dialogues short and succinct. Limit each dialogue to a single main thought. Try to restrict each character to about three lines of dialogue at one time.

2. Use context clues to hint at the topic of your characters' conversation. For example, if two characters are speaking about an awkward topic such as breaking up, build the tension and discomfort of the scene by describing their body language, e.g., a male and a female lingering on the front porch, not saying much, keeping their arms folded. When the male eventually suggests, "What if we just tried living separately?" the dialogue will provide resolution of the tension.

3. Vary your format when creating dialogue tags. Avoid a series of, "He exclaimed," followed by "She sneered," "He gasped," and "She interjected." One way to tell if you're writing good dialogue is to ask yourself, "Will my reader know my character is acting surprised, angry, or hyper without me saying so in a tag?" The real purpose of a dialogue tag is to help your reader keep track of who is talking. The use of too many descriptive verbs in this situation can actually distract from the conversation.

If you can make it obvious which character is talking, then you do not need a tag at all. For example: "I can't believe he's late." Jessie continuously checked her watch. "He said eleven thirty." You also do not need tags if you indicate that two characters are speaking and then continue their conversation without an action break.

4. Do, however, break up your dialogue with action so that it does not run on too boringly. By doing this you can minimize dialogue tags while providing your reader with enough details for an accurate visualization.

5. give your dialogue the correct punctuation. If you don't, your reader can easily become confused and give up on your book. Here are three simple rules to remember:

- Always add a comma between the end of your dialogue and a tag line ("My parents are so lame," Emily said).

- Keep the comma or period inside the quotation marks.

- Use a comma at the end of the first section of an interrupted statement and another comma at the end of the tagline. ("I don't know," Emily said, "We'll just have to wait and see.").

Chapter 4: What's The Point?

So you have an idea for a book. That's usually the first thing that happens in the process of writing one. Many first-time authors think that all they need is one good idea in order to write an engaging, exciting tale; however, having an idea is only the first step. Before you can even start writing, it helps to have an inkling about the point of your story. An idea essentially says "somebody does something interesting" or "something exciting happens," but an idea is not a fully fleshed out novel. After you come up with your idea, you'll need to start filling in the blanks. Who is that somebody? What happens that is so exciting? This chapter is all about how to figure that out.

The goal of a story is often echoed in the protagonist's goal, so it only makes sense to first figure out what your protagonist wants. Think about internal and external goals and how conflict can play into them. Let's say that you have an idea to write a book about pirates that actually do good instead of evil. That's your idea. Now you have to fill in the blanks and flesh out the details. Say there is one pirate named Johnny, he's your protagonist and he is the one who is behind this change in behavior. Why? Maybe because he met a girl and wants to exit the life of a pirate. We can add conflict by providing background information that explains when Johnny first became a pirate, he took a lifelong vow; now a fellow pirate is determined to prevent Johnny from weaseling out of his promise. See how the fleshing out process works? The story goal in this case could be something like, "escape evil and live free."

Here are some examples of classic story goals that you might be able to work into your idea:

Escape From Something

In many stories, the protagonist's goal is to escape from something, whether from the antagonist, an opposing force, a mistake, or any other circumstance The storyline in the novel *Safe Haven* is about a woman attempting to escape from her psychotic husband by moving to another town. In *Hansel and Gretel*, the siblings try to escape from the evil witch before they get killed. In the TV show *Prison Break*, one of the main characters escapes from prison with the help of his brother and other inmates. Sometimes a character just wants to escape from reality, as in *The Wizard of Oz*.

Gain Money

Just as money is a prominent topic in real life, so it is also often a factor in many story goals. The idea of gaining money often motivates people (and characters). In the movie *The Glass House*, the antagonists, Terry and Erin, are motivated to kill off their two godchildren so they can inherit four million dollars. Many storylines involving money involve greed and often they have crime-related undertones, but in some cases a story goal about gaining money can be positive.

For example, you could write a story in which your protagonist has a goal to raise money for something important, but then obstacles and challenges kick in...remember those plot twists!

Defeat the Villain and Save the Townspeople

One of the most common story goals in existence is to defeat the bad guy, which often equates to saving the townspeople. This often comes with the "good versus evil" theme. In *The Lord of the Rings*, Frodo had to defeat Gollum and all the forces that would destroy him and take the ring. In *Spiderman*, Spiderman has to defeat several villains who are out to destroy the town. In *The Wizard of Oz*, Dorothy is tasked with defeating the Wicked Witch of the West. More often than not, the protagonist wins against the villain but you can always twist it the other direction. Sometimes the villain ends up winning in the end, such as in the movie, *No Country for Old Men*.

Survive in a Foreign Environment

Surviving a foreign environment is another common story goal of many books. Survival storylines can be found in the TV shows such as *Lost* and *Gilligan's Island*. There are many classic tales about being stranded on a desert island, stuck in a foreign country, or abandoned on another planet. Sometimes this story goal can be reversed, assigning as protagonists aliens or monsters who are stranded on Earth. For good examples of this reversal, see the movie *Coneheads* or *My Favorite Martian*. It is easy to develop a double conflict with a story goal like this, because the characters often grow attached to the foreign environment after a while, but still want to return home. You can easily string this conflict out until the very end of the book if you want, making it difficult to tell which desire will win out in the end.

Win a War

Winning a war is a highly actionable and greatly exhilarating story goal when it is about war or battle itself. There have been countess storylines with a goal of winning a war against another country, another race, another species, etc. Winning a war can mean winning a sports war, a workplace war, a political war, a racial war, or a relationship war. A story goal about winning a war can also be metaphorical, such as winning the war against a disease, poverty, or crime. In *The War of the Worlds* by H. G. Wells, the goal of mankind is to defeat the alien invaders. In *Alien v. Predator*, it's a battle between two species. In a storyline with a goal of winning a war, there is usually something valuable at stake if one side does not win.

Clear Your Name

A wrongly condemned victim of the justice system is almost certain to win the sympathies of your readers, making this story goal one of the more interesting to pursue. This story goal almost comes ready-made with a number of possible conflicts from which to choose. There is enough variety to select from among criminal settings, identity theft, or any number of interesting story goals. Storylines like this often contain undertones of politics or betrayal.

Protect Something of Value

When a character's goal is to rescue or protect someone or something that is highly valuable, the story is often suspenseful and exciting by its very nature. Often the stakes are raised by adding one or more antagonists who are competing for the same "asset." This injects an element of time urgency and increases the danger exponentially.

Sometimes the protagonist who is doing the protecting is motivated by a past failure. In the movie *Mercury Rising* (based on the book *Simple Simon*), Bruce Willis gets deeply involved in protecting an autistic 9 year old; Willis is driven internally because he had let another young kid get killed on his watch in a previous job.

Love

Love is a very broad story goal because it can branch off into many different subtopics. A story goal about love could be a character trying to get two people to connect, forbidden love (such as in *Romeo and Juliet*), interracial love (such as in *Othello*), unexpected love (*Labor Day*), ill-advised love, unconditional love, a love triangle, etc. Love is a universal emotion, so it is a very popular and engaging story goal.

Settle a Debt

Sometimes the story goal of a character is to settle an old debt. For example, you'll have a protagonist who is just living his life and all of sudden, an old friend from the past shows up wanting help; of course your protagonist happens to be in debt to the friend. In another scenario, your protagonist could be in trouble and needing help; he gets help, but only because his rescuer is indebted to him. In the movie *We're the Millers*, the main character is forced to steal drugs from Mexico for a client because he owes the client a large amount of money and he can't find another way to gain forgiveness.

If a main theme is clear, then keep it in mind when working on your story goal; your goal will often have a connection or some relevance to the primary theme. Your theme can be compared to the moral or the lesson of the story. Here is a list of some of the most common topics that relate to themes found in books:

- Betrayal
- Heroism

- Capitalism
- Identity Crisis

- Change versus Tradition
- Chaos and Order
- Coming of Age
- Darkness and Light
- Death
- Displacement
- Empowerment
- Faith and Doubt
- Family
- Fate versus Free Will
- Fear
- Good versus Evil
- Greed and Materialism
- Immorality
- Lost Love
- Man versus Nature
- Motherhood
- Overcoming a Weakness
- Person Against Society
- Power and Corruption
- Racism
- Sacrifice and Love
- Self-Awareness
- Simplicity
- Social Injustice

Your theme can range from the very simple to the emotionally or intellectually deep. Either way, it should represent a truth about the world.

If a theme does not immediately present itself, go ahead and start writing. Your theme, or themes, will eventually surface. If you want additional clarification on story themes, a YouTube video by Mistersato411, entitled, How to Find a Theme, may prove helpful.

Chapter 5: Build A Framework

Writing a book can be overwhelming, especially if it's your first time. The good news is that you can pretty easily get a handle on the big picture and maintain continuity across hundreds of pages–using outlines. I recommend that you outline, not just the story itself but each major aspect: the plot, your characters, the chapters, and scenes within those chapters. With these aspects outlined, you are able to easily access and reference the most important parts of your story.

While some writers depend heavily upon outlining to get them through the writing process, others hate outlines and firmly resist their use. Managing via outlines is a personal preference, but I think you can benefit from this discipline, especially in the beginning. Don't begrudge yourself the time it takes; the process of outlining multiple aspects of your story will actually help ensure you don't miss important details. By the time you have completed your outlines, you will be fully prepared to start the actual writing.

The best way to approach outlining is with an open, flexible mind. Outlines can feel rigid, but they're not intended to trap or confine you–their purpose is to give you a big-picture view of your story; in that way, they can actually reduce your stress. Think of an outline as a roadmap; it's meant to guide you along a specific route, but that does not mean you are forbidden from taking side trips along the way. I like outlines because they help me test how far I can develop my ideas. If I outline an idea and see that I can take it really deep, then I know it's worth developing further. If I can't really flesh out an idea, then I know not to waste my time on it. Outlines can help prevent dead-ends in your plot as well as ensuring consistency in your writing.

The Elevator Pitch

I like to start out my outline by defining the storyline in one to three sentences. Pretend you're crafting an elevator pitch about your book. It should be short but packed with enough interesting details to stop people in their tracks.

First, describe your protagonist, either by name (if a well-known person) or by personality. Unless your protagonist is a household word, you should stick to generic terms in your storyline sentence. For example, if you had a protagonist named Stanley who was a loner, you would omit the name and just describe him as a loner. However, if your first book was a hit and you are now building a series upon it, by all means capitalize on the name recognition and thereby connect your readers to this new release.

Include:

- The situation at the beginning of the story and your protagonist's goal

- The first plot twist or obstacle and the conflict that follows

- A mention of the antagonist

Here is an example of a storyline:

When a depressed loner (the protagonist) finally finds the woman of his dreams (the current situation), he vows to love her for life (the goal). But when this girl (the antagonist) falls for another man (the first plot twist or obstacle), the loner refuses to let go, stopping at nothing–not even revenge–to get her back (the conflict).

The Synopsis

After the summary, you will write your book's **synopsis.** A synopsis is a brief sketch of your storyline. You should always write your synopsis in the third person and using the present tense. Start with your plot outline, then expand upon it to create a story synopsis in a maximum of two pages. Touch on each plot twist and include major story events.

The first step in writing a synopsis is to flesh out the beginning of your story. Keep in mind that this will be the first thing a prospective publisher will see. It also determines whether a reader will keep reading so skillfully insert your story hook and provide as much vivid action as possible. Highlight the first plot twist your protagonist encounters.

Next, summarize the middle of your story, highlighting the second and third plot twists. Toward the end of this section, you will summarize the events or issues that lead your characters toward their final confrontation.

Finally, sketch out the climax of the tale by describing its final conflict and showing briefly whether or not your protagonist achieves the desired objective. A solid synopsis will stand on its own, without needing further details. I encourage you to test your synopsis by asking someone who knows nothing about your story to read it and give you some feedback.

The Scene List

Another way to lay out your story is with a **scene list**. A scene list can provide a complete overview of your book in just a few pages, thus serving as a useful organizational tool. Scene lists make it easier to edit your book once you've finished. They assist you in identifying and deleting unnecessary scenes and can help you know exactly where is the best place to insert anything essential that has been overlooked.

To make a scene list, create a spreadsheet or a table with six columns. Label these columns "Scene Name," "Characters," "Point of View," "Location,"

"Summary," and "Moves Plot Forward?" then, starting with the first row, fill in the information for the first scene. In the first column, give your scene a name or other identifier. Moving to the right, list each character that appears in the scene, followed by whose point of view is used, and the location of the scene. Then write a couple of sentences briefly summarizing how the scene progresses and write "Yes" or "No," based on whether or not the scene moves the plot forward. If it does not, then you may be able to omit the scene.

Each scene you write should be interrelated with the others and look to at least move toward answering the reader's questions and further development of the major themes of your book. For example, if you plan a scene in which your protagonist discovers he has a child he didn't know about, then you're going to need to set up the scene so your readers will say, "That makes sense." In this scenario, I would write an earlier scene where your protagonist and a respective character have a meeting where a secret could be revealed, but an argument breaks out and the secret is never told.

Some writers use flowcharts to portray the progression of their story. This involves using boxes to show movement from the exposition, to the rising action, on to the climax, and then to the resolution of your story. Boxes representing the development of themes usually run beneath the story flow.

 Pay special attention to the ending of your book. Your ending will be your last contact with the reader; in it you have one final opportunity to leave a lasting impression. Break down your ending into several scenes that build suspense and lead to a strong and memorable resolution. Sometimes I am so strongly aware of how I want to end a book that I'll write the ending first; then I will deconstruct the story backwards from the ending. This reverse-order process enables me to space out the prerequisite details across previous scenes, giving various levels of obscure hints as to what is to come.

If later I find that the ending just doesn't work, I can always change it. Never think your work is wasted when you need to delete whole sections. Writing is a process, usually a process of trial and error. Every step you take is necessary, even if it looks like you are wasting whole chapters full of hard work. Each idea you scrap helps eliminate the unnecessary so that you can discover the best path for your story. Some books are like that. They will demand to go places you did not foresee. No worry; you can always rewrite as needed. If you truly have no idea what kind of ending to write, set your work aside for a few days. When you come back to it, first read through everything you have written, looking for leads you can pursue that might take you to a satisfying ending. Often, just backing away briefly will add enough objectivity to clarify where your story wants to take you.

The Character List

In Chapter three we talked about making a character list to help stay organized. We discussed important questions *about* your character but omitted the character description itself.

You can describe your character throughout the story itself because that helps give your readers a mental picture but during the outlining process, I recommend making a very detailed description. Consider everything, including details about body language, facial features, expression, thought processes, etc. Put yourself in your characters' shoes and try to describe him from that point of view. I like to have one master document per story with each character listed on a separate page. Then I use an entire page to create an individual's profile. Sometimes I'll go really crazy and even decide where they go to school or where they work. Those details can unlock storylines like you'd never believe.

Help! I'm Stuck!

Finally, I love the outlining process because sometimes it helps me overcome writer's block. I'll be honest, if I have an idea, I'll often skip the outlining process and jump straight into sporadic writing and only return to the outline when I've encountered writer's block. As I said earlier, I believe the outlining process can be very inspiring and creative. With almost every story I've written, I've turned to outlining, at least eventually.

For example, writing a synopsis often helps me brainstorm ideas where the story goes to next. I might have my story written up the first plot point but then I'll be left clueless once I'm at the midpoint. At the first plot point, I can start asking myself, "Well what if..." and see if I can come up with a good midpoint scenario. I try to ask myself what my readers would and would not expect and pick the more exciting route (usually what they wouldn't expect). If I really cannot pick something, sometimes I'll invent a new character and find a way to work him or her in.

The outlining process also enables me to backtrack. If I'm writing a scene list and come across a scene that I think is boring, the outlining process allows me to go back and rework it rather than just scrapping it altogether. It also enables me to take a break from writing one scene and jump to another if I can't figure out where to take it.

Some other things you can do to help beat writers' block are to do some research for inspiration or experiment with switching point of view. Research sounds awful but sometimes it can be really fun! For example, I thought about writing a story about gangs, but I have no knowledge of gangs or how they work, so I read a memoir about gangs to get a better idea. Switching the point of view in a scene is more like a creative writing activity to help you gain a more rounded view of your story and characters.

Finally, I've always found that simply taking a break helps me. Sitting at a computer for long hours can be draining. I know that I usually get tired and hungry, so I'll go grab a bite to eat, do something fun for a little bit (maybe listen to music or watch a show), just get my eyes away from the screen and I'll usually come back feeling refreshed. I also always go back over the parts of the story I wrote as my tiredness was setting in because eight out of ten times I find that's where I start rushing and slacking off.

Chapter 6: Tips and Strategies

Keep a Writing Journal

Writing is a skill and a form of self-expression. We can develop the skill throughout the course of our lives and we deepen our writing as we grow into ourselves. Written expression is like a muscle; if you don't use it, you will lose it. I find whenever I take an extended writing break, that when I start up again my skills will be rusty. My inspiration will be slow in coming and my ideas will be limited; I will have lost my edge when it comes to punctuation and writing dialogue.

Some of the best advice I have received is to write something, *anything* at least once a day. Even if you don't write anything related to an actual story, you should write, just to keep your skills honed and ready for use. I personally maintain a daily handwritten journal. It forces me to write at least a little every day, keeping my writing mind sharp. It not only enables me to practice writing, but also helps me document my life.

Turn Negative Energy into Words

If you are upset or agitated, write down your feelings instead of taking them out on somebody else. I have avoided many regrettable incidents this way, sometimes even writing my way back to a state of peace, other times writing until I have uncovered a possible resolution to the situation. Expressing your feelings on paper can serve as your daily writing exercise and who knows, it might even lead to a great story in the future. Use your negative energy positively!

Learn from your Competition

The world of writing is full of competition—even more so since self-publishing became respectable and e-books emerged as a thriving business. Self-publishing and e-book releases allow just about anybody to publish a book. The proliferation of new material can sometimes be overwhelming.

Instead of losing heart, choose to *learn* from other successful writers. Don't waste your time and energy on jealousy or a critical spirit. Instead of competing, look to learn from others. I often will buy another writer's best-seller in order to research what made the book so successful. I read reviews, watching for common touch points among the readers. I never view other authors as direct competition, simply because I learn so much from them.

Your writing is an expression of your unique person. In that sense, you *have* no competition. If you find yourself reacting to the work of others with anger or other negative emotions, it may be an indication that you are unsure of yourself. Either you haven't figured out who you are, or you are doubting the validity of your message. However, the more you grow into yourself, the clearer will be your voice and the more willing you may be to risk sharing your unique viewpoint.

Most writers acknowledge that writing is a constant growing process and are quite willing to discuss what they are learning along the way. The strange thing is, even though writing is a solitary activity, writers need other writers. They need a safe community in which to "talk shop" or field new ideas to get feedback. Our work is so subjective that we occasionally need the help of a more objective set of eyes. For these reasons, I highly recommend seeking out a writers' group.

Write with Heart

Put your heart into whatever you're writing. Write about what you're truly thinking about deep in your heart. Stories that are written straight from your heart often have a natural flow that captures your readers' attention. Passionate writing rarely sounds forced and if you've been writing for a while, the story will sound even more amazing.

Don't Quit Until You Finish

Writing a story is hard work and it can be tempting to give up halfway through. When I wrote my first book, I nearly gave up after six months and thought I would never finish; then something deep within told me to keep going. I'm glad I persevered, because within a few more months, I had self-published my first book! It may seem hard, but if you just keep working your way through the tough spots, the final result will feel great. Don't rush yourself. It only takes some writers a few months to write a book, where it can take others years. Work at your own pace. One thing I have learned is to never rush. Sometimes I think I rushed my first book; now I wonder what would be the end product if I had taken it slower.

Edit Well

Editing your book is another one of the most important steps in the world of writing. Editing is what allows you to go over your first and subsequent drafts and make it perfect for your readers. Many writers make the mistake of editing as they go along. I think that editing is best saved until after the first draft of your book is written; it allows you to write passionately focus on raw thought. I know lots of writers who are tempted to go back and edit after writing a paragraph or a chapter but I think that takes away from my true words.

Develop Your Style

There are many ways to figure out and develop your writing style. Your writing style might cause your opinion to shine through or it might be rhythmic. Your sentence structure and length could differ and your tone can be distinct. You can use lots of literary devices or write in a more straight-forward manner. Some authors, like William Faulkner, use the stream of consciousness style (where the story is written through a character's conscious thoughts). Some authors love writing in present tense and others might even be as daring as to write in second person. You might even write fiction in the form of a frame tale. Your writing style may start out as one thing and develop into a new style. The best way to develop your style is to write and keep writing!

Write Simply

Be careful not to write too elaborately. Avoid using too many adjectives, adverbs and flowery descriptions–especially about your setting. If something can be turned into dialogue, do not let it get lost in a paragraph. Keep your sentences short and concise. Writing too elaborately will not only turn off your readers, but it will turn publishing agents away as well. That being said, you can still use literary devices such as similes and metaphors, just use them in a simple, easy-to-read context. You can also be descriptive, just use description for a purpose, to paint a picture in your readers' minds.

Subplots

A subplot is an additional plot in your story, structured in the same way, only on a smaller scale. Writers generally use subplots to strengthen the main plot. Subplots should be concluded before the actual conclusion of your story. They can involve your protagonist or a minor character. Here is an example of a plot with a subplot: A gangster has to execute a hit job for his gang (main plot) while also dealing with disciplining his kids, who are acting out (subplot). Not every story needs a subplot but it can definitely be helpful in turning a shorter story into a longer story. Subplots can also add variety to your story and help keep your readers interested.

Since adding subplots to your story can be complex, I recommend treating each plot as a short story and then editing them in together during the editing process. This is where a scene list comes in handy, because you can easily give yourself an overview of each plot and organize each one as needed. Build each subplot as strong and as solid as if it were your main plot; otherwise it will weaken rather than strengthen your story.

Mental Pictures

If you're having trouble describing a character or scene, try closing your eyes and visualizing it before you write down as many details as possible. Pretend like you're watching a movie as you write. One time, I was writing a short story where the main character killed himself in the prologue. I've never experienced anything like that ever and had no idea how to portray that in written form. I checked YouTube for suicide scenes in movies to give me an idea how I could write it.

Experimenting With Dialogue

If you're not sure where to take your story, experiment by writing dialogue first. Don't assign specific dialogue tags or even indicate who is speaking. Just start with a piece of dialogue and see where it goes. Add conflict to make it even more interesting. If you like what you came up with, then see about assigning each line to a character.

Back in the olden days, when AOL Instant Messenger was popular, I used it to carry on many conversations with my friends. I didn't know the program actually kept a copy of every conversation I had until I accidentally discovered them on my computer. After reading through some of my conversations, I was able to take some of the dialogue and work it into my current book. In fact, I took an entire fight I had with an ex just before we broke up and was able to create the break-up scene in one of my books by giving my characters lines from the conversation. Of course, I changed the names to protect the "innocent."

Choose the Unusual

One of the best things about fiction writing is that you can exercise your creativity muscle and experiment with things until you come up with something really good. For example, if you're having trouble thinking of a memorable character, try experimenting with gender norms. You might be writing about a construction worker, a role that is stereotypically masculine, but try writing it for a female construction worker–something much more surprising and memorable. Do this for all the aspects of your story if you're feeling stuck, and see what you can come up with.

Take a Break

I mentioned this in an earlier chapter, but I will stress again that it is very important to take breaks in between writing. I've never heard of an author who just sat down and wrote a perfect story straight through. You will experience challenges and obstacles just like your protagonist. Your eyes will get tired, your wrists will grow sore, you might run out of ideas, etc. Taking a break can help you refresh your mind and creativity. You can take a short break or a long break (I once took a 6 month break). As long as you love writing, your heart will bring you back to it eventually.

Colorful Words

Writing is an art, so don't be afraid to write poetically. Experiment with literary devices such as metaphors, similes, ironies, and satire. My favorite literary device is similes. I love comparing events in my stories to another item. I believe that it helps my readers enhance their senses when reading my works. For example, see how this simile works: As his mouth grew drier, his tongue felt *like sandpaper* on a rough surface. I also like to include metaphors, because they enhance the readers' ability to visualize a scene. Here is a good example of a metaphor: Ari did such an unorganized job of inventory at her job that she left the back room *a disaster area.*

Open with a Bang

Avoid opening your book with a scene where everybody is happy and at rest. Instead, drop in some sort of disturbance. For example, if your story opens on a family with young kids, make one of the kids cry instead of play. Or have the couple at the door argue instead of kissing each other goodbye. Add something exciting and attention-grabbing. This will make your readers ask, "Why is x happening?" and they'll want to read more. This is especially helpful when a prospective reader picks up your book in a library or bookstore and reads the first few pages prior to making a decision to read or buy the book.

No Weather, Please

For some reason, many new writers tend to open a story with a description of the weather. "It was a dark and stormy night." or "The sun shone down on the hot, humid summer day." I've been guilty of opening up with the weather, but now that it's been brought to my attention, I can see why it sounds cliché. It's ultimately *your* story and you can open it up however you want. However, I've heard that opening up with the weather scares the publishing agents away in a heartbeat. So, if you're writing a story with publication in mind, I recommend avoiding a straight up weather description. Of course, you could always find a way to work the weather in. A good strategy is to connect it to your character's viewpoint. You might be able to even drop it in through the use of a simile or metaphor.

In Tense

The two most common tenses for writing are the past tense and present tense. The past tense third person novel is by far the most popular. Although a story written in present tense has its benefits, readers are often just more used to it than anything else.

The present tense enables you to communicate immediacy to a reader. It also enables you to write in a stream of consciousness if you want to. But present tense also limits your ability to manipulate time, create complex characters, and take away from the suspense factors. Like many book writing decisions, the tense you decide to use is ultimately up to you.

Use First Person Carefully

Writing in the first person can be easy and intimate as opposed to the third person. First person writing can enable you to easily stay in one viewpoint throughout your story. It can also feel as if the narrator is sitting right next to the reader. On the other hand, some writers feel that writing in first person limits their ability to tell the story from a broader perspective, because it can only be told through the eyes of one character.

Write What You Know

The easiest way to write a successful story is to write about what you know. A friend worked in a fast food restaurant for six years and was therefore able to write an accurate and hilarious musical about a fast food restaurant. Anybody who has never worked in fast food would have been able to give the same musical the authenticity of my friend. Many famous authors have purposefully put themselves in situations to gain experience for a story. One author spent time in a mental institution to be able to write authentically within that setting . Having experienced something for yourself makes it a million times more authentic when you write about it. This is why so many professors and experts easily get published in the non-fiction world; they write about their field of expertise. You can do the same with fiction. If my friend were to novelize her musical about fast food, take it to a publisher, and say "I spent six years in the fast food industry," she would stand a much higher chance of getting published than if she wrote from her ignorance about rocket science.

Read Out Loud

Reading your story out loud to yourself is a helpful editing tool. You catch mistakes more easily when you hear them and you can more easily confirm that the rhythm of your sentences feels okay. Of course, if you're writing a long novel, I would break it into sections to read out loud; reading a two hundred page book out loud in one setting will be hard on your voice, not to mention your mind.

Choose Your Title Wisely

Sooner or later, you'll have to pick a title for your story. This may sound easy but as I've recently discovered, it can be a very daunting task, requiring strategy and knowledge of the market. A title is everything; it tells your readers what the story is about and catches their eye at first glance. Your title has to sound impressive enough to evoke curiosity. It cannot be dull or boring, just as the story inside cannot be boring. When I was in the seventh grade, we were reading The Red Badge of Courage by Stephen Crane in English class. I remember my teacher telling us that Crane originally named his book something boring like, "The Trials of Henry," The publishers, however took the title right out of his own text. Now, which title sounds better to you? Choosing the right title can be tricky but luckily there are some things you can consider to pick the best choice.

The title of your story should be appropriate and not misleading. For example, a title called "The Mystery Lovers" may sound to you like a romance but it might actually be about people who love to solve mysteries. The title should also be easy to remember. Memorable titles often come in the form of popular expressions, a play on words or a phrase borrowed from an existing work. For example, Faulkner's *The Sound and the Fury* came from a line in Shakespeare's *Macbeth*. A title can include your protagonist's name if it is memorable and significant. For example, Forrest Gump is memorable because of its uniqueness. The title of your book can represent a place, as in *The Glass House,* or it can be possessive such as *Edner's Game.* If you're writing a series, you could come up with a pattern for your title, The *Harry Potter* series has a repeating structure for each title.

One thing I've learned along the way is that it doesn't help to become too attached to your titles. You may like a specific your title because it means something special to you, but it won't help your cause if readers don't make the same connection. To maximize your chances of getting published and making some money, you will need to overcome this obstacle. I've found it helps to put my "pet" title on my first draft. I get to have, a fun fact, and anybody who loves my book will enjoy asking about the details of my working title.

Finally, you are unable to copyright a title, so legal problems won't be an issue. However, it is a good idea to research the title you want to give your book; if you accidentally use the same title as an already published book, you will have a much easier time getting published under an alternative.

Chapter 7: Light Bulb Moments

In order to write fiction, you will need an idea. If you're already a writer, I bet somebody has asked you where your idea came from. Ideas are strange things. Sometimes they hit a writer like an eighteen-wheeler out of nowhere; other times finding one is more like pulling teeth! I know many writers who base their stories off real life events and then give them a twist. The truth is, in most cases, coming up with your big idea is a process. I mentioned earlier that sometimes I get inspired by watching movies or playing video games. It can be different for everyone, but there are a few universal strategies you can use to get started. In this chapter, you will discover how you can generate ideas and possibly start writing the world's next best-seller.

One very useful strategy for generating ideas is to write on a single, small concept. Remember in Chapter six when I discussed how important it is to write something, anything every day? That's because even if you write about something random, it could actually turn into a useful idea. In doing this, you will have to exercise your creativity muscle but that will only help it grow stronger. For example, you could go sit on a park bench, observe your surroundings, and start writing about one of the people you see. Just write, write and keep writing. If you like what you come up with, keep spending time on it. If you don't like where it's going, scrap it and start over.

When I was younger, I used to have wild dreams that often became the basis for my stories. As an adult, I now keep a dream journal next to my bed with a pen so I can write about any dreams I remember as soon as I wake up, before I forget them in the busy rush of the day. You can use almost any dream or dream fragment as a jumping off point. Just start writing and see if you can develop any new ideas from there. You might not get a whole story idea from a dream but you might get a character or an idea for a plot twist. The protagonist for my friend's first self-published book came to her in a dream.

For those who tend to have ideas hit them out of nowhere, I recommend keeping a small notepad with you so you can write the ideas down as they come. Your idea may be so incredible that you think you won't forget it, but it's easy to forget even incredible ideas when you've got a lot going on all around.

Another way to generate ideas is to observe something and then ask why. For example, "Why is that big brick building abandoned?" "Why is it sitting in the middle of a small residential neighborhood?" Perhaps the building was once used as a secret-agent hide out and they built it in the middle of a residential neighborhood thinking that nobody would expect to find secret agents there. As with of the use of the female construction worker, allow your creativity free rein and see what emerges.

Here are a few things you can focus on to stimulate creative ideas:

Heroes and Heroines

Many fiction books revolve around a courageous hero or heroine, somebody who is quite brave–perhaps a knight in shining armor or a ruthless bounty hunter–and is out to save the townspeople and defeat evil. Traditional heroes and heroines often appear in fantasy books and fairy tales although you can also rework them into suspense thrillers and other genres. Readers like to read about heroes and heroines, because they often represent admirable qualities such as courage, determination, sacrifice, and valor.

Traps and Villains

Villains and their traps often coexist with heroes and heroines, because they serve as the antagonistic factors in a story. There is usually a villain behind a trap or obstacle that slows down the hero, serving as a huge plot twist. Traps can be simple, such as a hole in the ground covered by dirt, or elaborate, such as the villain sending out a decoy to lure the hero into danger. Your villain can be straight up evil or she can be the type who pretends to be good but is really not; of course, the protagonist usually doesn't figure this out until it's almost too late.

Encounters

Encounters are another great aspect of fiction story ideas. An encounter with something or someone can turn into a major plot twist. For example, the violent encounter where Oedipus kills another traveler ultimately leads to the fulfilled fate of killing his father and marrying his mother. In *The Wizard of Oz*, Dorothy encounters both friends and enemies who help drive the plot forward. I highly recommend working in some sort of encounter, be it friendly or hostile, into your story as a plot twist.

Incredible Items, Treasures, and Chases

Incredible items are often at the heart of a really good plot. A story about an incredible item usually consists of a protagonist trying to do the right thing with it and the antagonist trying to take it for the wrong purposes. In *The Lord of the Rings*, The Ring was the incredible item. In *The Wizard of Oz*, the ruby slippers were the item of interest. Writing a story about an incredible item or treasure usually enables you to work in heroes and villains and maybe even some traps. The story question is usually, "Will the hero succeed in protecting the item?" or "Will the hero find the treasure before the bad guys do?" These stories often involve a chase after the valuable item or a race to find the treasure first. Chases add to the suspense factor of your story. They can be high-action chases (such as the cops vs. robbers type) or they can be more slow and drawn out (such as the wicked witch showing up wherever Dorothy goes in Oz).

Amazing Machines

Machines can inject an element of the unexpected into your fiction story. Items to start with are time machines, flying machines, robots with special talents, or UFOs. Science fiction or fantasy stories often center on incredible machines. A plot twist for a story using machines could include the machine going haywire and wreaking havoc. A villain could be out to steal the machine and use it for evil purposes. The machine's malfunction could also put the protagonist in an awkward or dangerous situation. The possibilities are almost endless.

Hazards

Hazards have recently gained popularity via the current "end of the world" trend in storytelling. Hazards include natural disasters such as hurricanes, tornados, avalanches, lightning storms, and tsunamis. Hazards can also include cataclysmic events such as a meteor on a collision course with the earth, a sun burning out or growing too large, a volcanic eruption, the tearing of Earth's plates, or even alien invasions. Stories about hazards tend to fall into the category of science fiction. They are good for setting up a healthy suspense factor that has your readers asking, "Will Earth make it through this disaster?

Secrets

Secrets are useful for provoking interest and piquing curiosity. Secrets often lie at the heart of mystery and suspense novels. Either the protagonist has to solve a puzzle and unravel a secret, or he discovers a secret that changes his entire life. The antagonist could be holding a secret that would really affect the protagonist. Secrets can emerge within almost any genre of writing. They can be good, bad or a mixture. A secret may be hinted at throughout your book, building suspense until you reveal it at the very end of your story, to the thunderous applause of your readers.

Lost Civilizations

Lost civilizations allow you to fill them with creative detail and then take them down any path you want. You could give the people in your lost civilization special skills or unknown languages you can make them the keepers of an obscure secret wisdom, or make them the repository of a unifying principle behind the universe. You can write to almost any genre with a lost civilization. Because they are pretty much pure fiction, lost civilizations present a huge blank canvas for creative thinkers to fill. You can generate a unique backstory to explain the existence of the people, how the civilization came to be lost, and how it managed to survive. And then you get to gradually reveal its secrets to your reading audience.

Monsters

Monsters are a story topic that has been around for generations. Stories about vampires, werewolves, zombies, and mythical creatures have existed for millennia. Monsters can be good or scary, human-like or quite alien, both in appearance and in values. Monsters can work well in horror and suspense genres. Stephen King is best known for horror stories revolving around monsters. King has even made an innocent-looking clown into a deadly creature. Freddie Kruger was a normal guy until something happened to transform him into a monster. Monster stories are great for invoking fear in readers of all ages.

Diseases

Disease-based stories have followed the "end of the world" trend that has taken media by storm of late. There has been a recent skyrocket in apocalyptic stories involving zombies and other parasites. Although I personally think zombie and disease storylines are becoming terribly overused, there is still room for a creative twist to the old clichés. A disease can also be something more health-related. Perhaps you write a story about a new type of disease that you can spread by sneezing, so your protagonist has to find a way to prevent sneezes. Don't limit your mindset to zombies when you hear "disease." Branch out and really be creative in this category.

Fights

Stories about fights or wars are good for showing action and building suspense. Conflict is a natural part of these works; it comes built in. Fights and wars can be provoked between groups of humans, between humans and monsters, humans and machines, humans and aliens, or between multiple species. A fight story can also consist of an internal conflict, within a person, between conflicting values or desires. War stories usually contain an epic climax where readers find out which side wins, making the final chapter especially important.

Moral Quandaries

Giving your protagonist a moral quandary is great for creating a story with a solid "person versus self" conflict. The moral quandary can be about anything, but to maximize your story's marketability, try to make it relevant to modern society. For example, your protagonist could be placed in a position to choose between spending a million dollars for a noble cause (say, to obtain a life-saving treatment of his sick little girl) or returning it to the wealthy person who dropped it. Readers will often read to the end to find out which path the protagonist has taken.

Religion and Politics

Religion and politics have inspired many stories across centuries of English Literature. Recently, *The Da Vinci Code* emerged with religious undertones. Earlier the book *1985* communicated a major political message.

Locations

Your story idea can stem from a city or town, whether already existing or completely original. You could write about a major city, such as New York and give it a twist. Perhaps it never rains in the city anymore, creating a major obstacle for the residents. You can write about your own neighborhood, but populate it entirely with ghosts. Your location could be as mundane as Everytown, or it could be set on Saturn. The story doesn't have to center around a specific city but it could start there, opening even more doors for creativity and a unique plot.

Traveling

Traveling is a great basis for a story idea. There are all sorts of traveling – time traveling, hiking, road trips, and stories set on airplanes, boats, trains or buses. Time travel often falls into the category of science fiction, but other types of travel have the ability to fit into almost any fiction genre. Where is your protagonist's destination? Why did she take this type of transportation? Will she experience any disasters, obstacles, or delays en route?

Chapter 8: The Grand Finale

You've probably heard enough about the first-half of your book–how important it is to start out fast, hook your reader, and hold their attention. What about the other half of your book, the ending? The ending is important for two primary reasons: It will influence whether readers buy another book by you and it will leave your reader with some sort of conclusion to the story question. Writing a story can be difficult and tiring, but once you've come to the end, you don't want to stop too early. If you quit before mastering the ending, all of your hard work may go flying out the door! In this chapter, you will learn how to write a compelling ending that can you're your readers eager to get their hands on your next book.

Rule #1: Reflect Your Theme in the Ending

Does the conclusion of your book reflect the theme of your book? Readers usually like to feel the theme at the end. For example, if your protagonist gives up his Wall Street job to marry the love of his life in the end, it could reinforce the implied theme that money does not buy happiness.

Rule #2: Bask In the Pleasure

By all means, you're allowed to have a happy ending. In fact, I encourage you to have a happy ending. But don't dump your ending suddenly on your readers, or you will leave them hanging. Detail your happy ending and lead up to it. Don't just say "Harry's family lived happily ever after." That can be very unsatisfying to your readers. If you've written dynamic characters, they'll want more closure than that. Account for what happens to each major character. Then, give your readers time to wallow in the warmth of a wonderful ending.

Rule #3: What Readers Expect

Although fiction writing is called fiction for a reason, sometimes your reader expects a certain type of ending based off the genre you've written. For example, a person who is reading a romance novel would probably be annoyed if the two love interests in the story didn't get together in the end. A person reading a mystery novel would probably leave a bad review if the mystery wasn't solved. You have the freedom and power to make any ending you want. Just be cognizant of what your audience is expecting.

Rule #4: Write a Satisfying Surprise Ending

Surprise endings are a great way to get a shock out of your readers, but you must write them in a strategic manner. Surprise endings are usually satisfying when the reader isn't able to predict them, but to be successful, do some foreshadowing throughout your book; drop hints so that, in the end, your reader can say "Oh, *that's* why the author said that, back there," and be content. One thing I've learned in my experience is that if you're going to create a huge shock at the end of your book, make it a satisfying shock. If it's something just randomly thrown in, your readers will not be happy.

Rule #5: Tie Up Loose Ends

One thing you want to avoid is to leave your reader hanging – unless your book is part of a series, in which it's okay to leave some issues unresolved. However, be sure that your reader can easily identify your book as part of a series. Even a simple "To Be Continued" disclaimer at the end will enable your readers to confirm that there's more to come. Otherwise, they may feel like their money has been wasted. The major reason your readers make it to the end is to see whether or not your protagonist reaches his goal. If you don't clarify whether or not that occurs, your readers will probably be quite disappointed and they may avoid reading a book by you in the future.   Readers want to see the result of your protagonist's growth at the end of your story. Show how he has become a better or person or how he has grown internally.

Rule #6: Write Unhappy Endings Carefully

Happy, positive endings are usually the norm for fiction stories, but some authors go the other direction to pen unhappy, negative endings. Negative endings can work, but they require careful attention and preparation. Readers may find an unhappy ending unrealistic and therefore may feel cheated of the fiction story experience.

Unhappy endings tend to require an amount of justification. If your protagonist dies in the end, your readers could have trouble accepting your ending. However, if your readers already knew he was suffering from a disease or if he died as a hero, in the process of saving the townspeople, they would probably feel satisfied. Just clue them into the risks before the story ends. If the unhappy ending just kind of hits them out of nowhere or proves unnecessary, your chances of reader satisfaction are split. Some readers absolutely love endings that take them by surprise and make them think, but other readers will trash your book for it. If you're going to have an unhappy ending, try to drop hints throughout your book so your readers aren't expecting something different.

Rule#7: On Writing Cliffhangers

Cliffhangers are useful in priming your readers to want more, ensuring a ready-made audience for the next installment in your book series. Your reading public will want to know what happens next, although it can be frustrating for them to have to wait until the next volume is released.   A well-written cliffhanger at the end of an amazing story can leave readers talking about it up until the next installment comes out. Here's how to write an amazing cliffhanger:

Obviously, save the cliffhanger for the end of your book. Your reader will have nowhere else to go after expecting a conclusion so this is good way to insert some shock factor. Sometimes authors leave small cliffhangers at the end of earlier chapters, but save the best cliffhanger, the one that will make readers go crazy, for last. If you do include a cliffhanger, make it quick and sudden. Don't allow your readers to see it coming. Then, in the next installment, immediately address the cliffhanger. Remember, your readers have been waiting a long time to have their questions answered. If you don't provide answers right away, you risk losing their interest and their readership for other books you release in the future.

Not sure how to write a cliffhanger? There are two strategies you can try. First, re-read some examples of cliffhangers in your favorite books and try to see how the author set them up. Then try to think of a cliffhanger that you would like to read in your book. Since you'll probably already know how your cliffhanger will end, ask a friend or family member to read your final chapter and see how well the cliffhanger works for them.

A Final Note on Endings

You can always write your ending first. This is usually how I write. If I have a strong idea, I tend to know how I want the story to end, so I write my ending first to capture my ideas in their rawest state. I always find that writing the ending first enables me to better set up my story as I write through it. However, sometimes I'm not sure of how I want the story to end. In that case, I will start writing and trust that the ending will make itself known later. If you write your ending first, remember that you can always go back and change it as needed. Nothing is ever set in concrete until your book is in print.

Conclusion

I hope this book was able to help you discover how to plan, set up and write amazing works of fiction.

Your next step is to develop an idea, then start planning your first book. If you don't have an idea to start off with, review your daily writing exercises, looking for one. After you've picked an idea you like, one you think has potential, the next thing to do is start outlining your book. This will serve as your guideline to writing the actual book.

The best way to do this is to keep your outline in a separate document. Open a blank page and label different sections for your storyline, the story goal and the story question. List your protagonists, antagonists and minor characters. Next, state the conflict, the theme and your story's genre. I then find it useful to outline the plot twists of the story using a three-act structure. I then begin to fill in the blanks, making changes until I have come up with a solid plot I like. I also recommend writing a synopsis so you will have a detailed but overall picture of where your story will go.

Once you have this roadmap, you can start to actually write your book! Set a goal for when you hope to finish, but remember that writing a successful fiction book may take longer than expected. Never rush, but work steadily; take the time you need to make it right. Then go back and edit your work until it's truly amazing!

Sneak Preview of The Angel's Blessing

Chapter 1 The Day of the White Rook

My Master did not become the great Warrior Shaman of peace because he was born with the blessings of the gods. He did not rise to his exalted place in the history of our worlds by the chance of ancestry, nor was he a child of fortune. He had no advantage other than his cunning, and he had no blessing other than that given to him by his grandfather. And that blessing was herb-lore.

My master was conceived and born in violence.

His mother was a young beauty who was ravaged by the invading Veylus pirates when our beloved city of Barnacle Atoll was overrun. When her time to give birth came, she held the newborn infant to her breast, the scrawny infant seeking to suckle a tit. But the nipple that the child found was cold and so he turned to his grandfather's thumb instead, and that thumb was hard and calloused and yet rich with the taste of mother-earth and her herbs. And so in his first suckle of life, the babe that was to be known simply as Kell, tasted the roots of us all.

Kell spent his youngest years under the domination of the brigands, and he quickly learned stealth and cunning as a way of life. In time, the Veylus were ousted by the armada of Queen Anastasias, and while her liberation was near devastation, the people of the Barnacles were once again free. With that freedom came years of reconstruction and tribute to the Queen, but that was far better than the pirates.

In that time Kell grew up as boys will. He was astounded with the world. His grandfather had a bountiful garden, and in there Kell saw crawlers and wigglers and flyers of all sorts. As a toddler, he tasted them and found them much crunchier than the wiggly ones of the root cellar. His grandfather often looked at him and sighed as adults will. But despite his odd tastes, he grew up healthy and strong.

Their small island of Dunsil wasn't on many sea-routes, but he and his grandfather were often visited by passing ships looking for a remedy to help a wounded or sick crewman. Often a boatful of sailors would come ashore and seek one of grandfather's special elixirs, and then ask of the ways with which to work the earth's gift. His grandfather never refused anyone in need -- for a fair price. Over the years, the legends grew of his incredible remedies. It was an ideal childhood and Kell was very happy.

Until the day that the Dorimans engulfed their island.

They were a gang of thugs with ships. Their fleet was small and fast and they would prey on defenseless lands, not to conquer, but to plunder and destroy. And before the Queen's forces could come to aid, they would sail away into the night's fog only to reappear in some other land, rough-handed and demanding. They wore no uniforms, and in their motley gear Kell saw them as something to be afraid of. He was a teenager at the time and the Dorimans saw him as a value to their number. And so at his grandfather's urging, he drew on all his cunning and he ran away.

He ran across the crest of the island and to the common ground where others were also gathering and afraid. Understanding his plight, the elders brought him to a cove with a light boat hidden within. They told him to sail straight to Angove's Cay, which was the home of Wendfala the Witch.

The young witch, seeing my Master's comely and youthful state, took him in and proceeded to teach him the ancient ways. It is said that in those dark hours while our very island writhed beneath the boots of the Dorimans, Wendfala made my Master into a man, and the young boy emerged from her clutches alert, able and with a new sort of strength that radiated off him like an aura.

They say that he emerged from her embraces as a magical paladin who single-handedly rallied the people and sent the Dorimans howling away and afraid. They say that he was the hero who liberated our islands and that the

Doriman still fear his name. And they say that when he was done with the Dorimans, the of battle was still upon him, and so he sailed the world in search of glory, wisdom and to inflict Holy Justice upon the wicked. For years sailors and merchants would land on our island and tell tales of Kell's valor in lands unknown.

That's what they say.

In the years of peace that followed many tales were told and retold, and then told and changed again and again. And in the small confines of the island of Dunsil the simple herbalist's grandchild became a living legend.

He returned to our island the year that I was born, and while many looked at the legendary hero in awe, their real amazement was that the lad looked as if he had never left. It was as though time had not touched him, and when he walked into his grandfather's cottage with his backpack full of magic and treasures, the old man simply looked up and told him that the garden needed tending.

He would say nothing of his adventures, but people would talk. Kell shunned their stories, but he didn't shun their company. He was still young and he had a quick wit at the tavern and loved winning at darts and skittles. The young women all eyed him and so at the festivals and dances he never lacked a partner. His knowledge of herbs and medicines grew as his grandfather taught him all he knew as he waned in years. People came to trust the young man as they did his old grandfather, sometimes more.

In time, the great herbalist finally passed. Every man woman and child on Dunsil stood on the white sands of the island's eastern shore as Kell made ready the last boat. They covered his body in beautiful flower blossoms, in hopes that the sea would pause and delight in the scent and so allow fair winds to carry him to his eternal paradise. Even the witch Wendfala came to give her blessing.

I was just a small boy at the time. I remember my mother urging me, my sisters and my brothers to let go of our flowers. But I was fascinated by the naked old man. He was nothing but old bones wrapped in tan skin at the bottom of a small rustic boat, and yet the blossoms made him seem almost alive.

"Forgive my child Kell," my mother said. "He is –"

"Young," Kell said. "And fascinated."

Then he set his gaze on me and he smiled.

It was not that long after the funeral that I was selected to be Kell's apprentice. I trembled with the honor and surged with excitement.

I had heard all of the grand tales. Indeed, I had been raised in the shadow of those magnificent stories, and when he and my father bartered for my apprenticeship, I thought that the gods themselves had blessed me.

"He's kind of scrawny."

"Yeah," my father said. "He is. But how much bulk do you need to scratch out your herbs?"

Kell frowned.

"Look," my father said. "I have a farm. Farming is a strong man's job. The boy will be better in your hands. I will give you milk, cheese and all the whey you want for four years."

"Seven."

I listened as they haggled over my worth. In the end I went for the price of six years of milk, three of cheeses and all the whey I could carry between the houses until I was seventeen.

It was a good bargain.

Master Kell was a soft-spoken and kindly man. He treated me well and our house wanted for nothing. Along with teaching me herb lore, he also taught me numbers and letters, and while I found numbers valuable in weighing and mixing and figuring out the price to put on a remedy, I never understood why Kell put so much value on writing.

We worked in a daily routine and there were always things to get done or learn. But Kell was a light-hearted soul and we often took the time to play. We would sometimes end a long day frolicking and fishing on one side of Crystal Lake while the women washed their laundry on the other. My master had an eye for the ladies and there were quite a few nights that I spent alone sleeping under the Starlight.

When I came into my teenage years I learned two very important lessons of life. One was girls. When I was young girls were simply giggly playmates, but as I matured I began to see those gigglers grow round, soft and firm, and that made me wonder. And there were odd things about my own body that I didn't understand; strange stirrings and desires. I asked my master about these feelings but he seemed somewhat at a loss, then smiled and assured me that all would be revealed in time.

I wondered about how long that time might be. And then one day a woman named Loleena came calling. She was from the other side of the island and I barely knew her. Kell graciously invited her to sup with us and the woman seemed to take an immediate interest in me. I was flattered that such a fine lady would even recognize my existence, let along talk with me.

The night was cool and getting cooler. Kell excused himself to gather more wood for the fire, but he didn't return till dawn. And that night Loleena helped me understand what it was like to be a man.

Over time I became an expert at herb lore and my master's special elixirs where in high demand, giving me plenty of practice at the craft. When it came time for the harvest festival, I was invited for the first time to join the adults around the big bonfire. There was music and dancing, and everyone cheered when Kell produced a keg of his special brew. The draught was sweet and heady and at first I didn't feel its effects. But then the festival started to feel a lot more happier to me. The dancing was lighter, the music was sweeter, and the young girls seemed prettier. The brew seemed to have the same effect on the girls as well, because they suddenly found me handsome. I did not lack for sweet company all that day and night.

Winters on the Atoll were usually cold and dreary. Work still needed to be done, but the sun would set earlier and earlier and the nights cooped up in the cottage could be wearisome. In those days I was glad to have learned my letters. My master had books on his craft and a boring volume entitled *The List of Leaves* that helped pass the dreary time.

We woke one chill sunny morning to a racket outside. Rooks were calling and crying. We rushed outside to see what was happening and the sky was nearly blotted out by their numbers. It was an amazing sight. Thousands of them were circling overhead. They seemed to be whirling in a vortex that narrowed closer and closer to the center eye, and in that eye I saw a single speck of white.

As we watched the birds became more and more frantic. The center mass of birds began to dip down and then formed into a funnel. I cried out and fell back to shield myself, but when they were only a few hundred feet above us a single rook parted from the myriad, spread its massive wings and began to descend. As it got closer we could see that the rook was as white as snow.

The pearlescent feathers seemed almost to gleam and its beak was like polished marble, but even as its spiny claws touched the sand of the earth the creature transformed. There stood before us a tall, bald man with skin as black as the night that seemed to almost shine blue where the sunlight fell on it. He was hairless from his head to his eyebrows and everywhere else a man should have hair. But what truly astonished me was that there was no manhood. At the place where his thighs met his pelvis there was nothing but smooth dark flesh.

"You are Kell," the man said in a silky, almost liquid voice.

“I am.”

And for all of my amazement and growing fear my master was as calm as the sea on a spring morning.

“I am an emissary from Wendfala,” he said. “The Witch calls on your pledge.”

There was a long pause before my master spoke. The birds above had wheeled out in a huge circle letting the sun shine onto us.

“Why doesn’t Wendfala come herself to call on this sacred pledge?” Kell asked in a powerful voice.

“She has been kidnapped,” the man-bird said.

“Kidnapped?” Kell bellowed, his hand unconsciously flexing as if to grab his weapon.

“She needs your help. In fact the whole of the Nine domains need your help.”

“With what? What is going on?” Kell asked with obvious concern in his voice.

“Wendfala calls for you. It’s not for me to judge her choice. I am only a messenger and ask you to hear her plea. I see smoke from your chimney. Can we go inside? It’s cold out here without feathers.”

“Um, sure. But first tell me, what is your name?” said Kell

“I am Byrinius.”

Kell motioned towards his house and as they turned to go inside Byrinius pointed towards me and asked who I was.

“This is Longo Nonan,” Kell said. “He is my apprentice.”

“Longo,” the man said. “Look at me boy. I have no hair and I have nothing where a human male should have something. But can you tell me what else there is about me that is not like you?”

At first I was frightened and my brain refused to work. But it felt as though the two would stare at me until I either flushed or fumbled like a child, or I solved the riddle. I looked. Then I looked again, and then I saw, but the words would not form and so I simply pointed to my belly.

"That's right," Byrinius said laughing long and hard. "I have no naval. I was not born, I was hatched. Kell, the lad is astute. Let him come with us and listen."

My master gave me a strange look, but I went with them and sat quietly in the corner. Kell offered tea but the man refused. He plucked a large ember from the fire, sat at the table, and held the glowing thing in his palm as he spoke.

"Visalth is coming," the man said.

As he spoke, vapors rose from the glowing ember. The smoke grew a little and then began to spin, then gather and spread into a wide sphere, and in the center of the sphere an image began to form. It was the image of a giant skeletal Dragon... A Bone Dragon.

I had heard of such things in stories, and in my youth they were terrifying. The mindless, soulless things would always seek to steal, kill and destroy and they could listen to no reason and had no fear for their own lives.

But these were modern times. Such myths were put away long ago along with frost fairies and trolls.

But that day my eyes had seen a bird transform into the vestige of a man who was now holding a scorching cinder in his hand as if it were a pebble, and the vision that formed in the room made me believe.

The dragon's bones were not like the white bleached things of men I had seen washed up on the beaches. They were deep brown like rotten teeth. It's long skull was swept back, flaring out into nine horns that turned forward like barbed fish-hooks. The hollow orbits were long, narrow and without eyes. It had a look of evil about it. I could not count the many spike-tipped vertebrae of the creature's neck, but the thing could wind and twist like a snake. Its ribs were slender, but what once had been the torso was long. Its fore-limbs grew from a solid breast-plate that looked scarred and beaten, and they were like a man's arms ending in grasping fingers. Its massive hind-legs bent like a deer, but the thighs could have been as thick as a trader ship's mast, and the claws could have crushed our house. The wings that sprouted from its back spread like enormous bird fingers, but between those bones there was no skin, only what looked like remnants of tattered sails or the clinging bits of flesh from creatures undreamed. The tail of the beast was easily as long as the whole creature, and as I watched the dragon fly about in the vision, the bony tail would whip back between the wings to attack like a scorpion.

"Magnificent," Kell said. "Truly a feat of powerful magic."

"Dark magic," Byrinius replied.

We watched the scene as the dragon lay waste to a solid castle set on a hill. The land was unknown to me. It was a lush place with rolling green grass, well cultivated farm land surrounded by walls and then a deep forest. But as we watched, the beast seemed to delight in wreaking ruin on the castle walls and buildings. An army of warriors looked helpless against the skeletal foe. Their arrows and bolts would bounce off the bones or sail through the empty spaces of its ribs. Even the catapults the men managed to muster had little effect, and they were quickly destroyed. When the undead horror had reduced the defenses to rubble it then turned on the army, sweeping men and cavalry away with its deadly tail.

"It seems bent on wanton destruction," Kell said.

"Not so. There is method in its madness. Observe."

I watched with a dull growing terror. When the army had been broken and the warriors were fleeing, men began to march in from the woods. The dragon seemed to suddenly heed some sort of call. It lifted and flew up on wings that were no wings, circling the walled city as the invaders easily took over.

"What are we seeing?" Kell asked. "What place is this?"

"It's Breakstone Hold, the Castle of Duke Venyez in Estile."

"Estile? That's in the Nine."

"It is," the man said. "It is on the Queen's western realms. The bone dragon's name is Visalth, and it's forces seem to be working their way along the alliance. Before Estile, the Duchy of Halnn fell. But the curious thing about the invasion is the pattern of assault. There is no warning, but just before an invasion all magic seems to disappear."

"What?"

"Wizards," the man went on, "witches, mages, even holy paladins seem to disappear. Whether these are physical or spiritual abductions I cannot say. But I do know that when Visalth appears there are none who can stand before him – they all disappear or get destroyed. And now Wendfala is captured, and from her prison she sends me to you ahead of the storm to get your aid."

Kell gulped his tea. The mystical scene vanished but Byrinius still held the glowing ember. My master stood and paced the room. He ran his fingers through his hair again and again. Then he finally stood before the window and gazed out to sea. He stood a long time. He then seemed decisive and strode to a locked wardrobe. He held his fingers over the handle and mumbled a quick verse. The doors popped open and from the inside he drew out a long and stout war-hammer that was glowing brightly.

The weapon was easily as long as my arm. Its handle was wrapped with red leather that showed stains of wear and sweat. The oaken shaft was carved in a hexagon. Cold blue steel ran from the crown down that shaft and was bolted with iron. The broad, flat head could easily have crushed an Ogres Skull, and the opposite side of the hammer was a nasty six sided piece of magical steel ending in a sharp point. The pommel was thick and ended with an 8 inch long double-bladed knife made of Admantium with a magically sharpened blade. Kell tossed his trusty weapon onto the table and the weight of it shook the table and dented it in several places.

"This is my little friend Ashrune," my master said. "How might we help?"

"You need to Flee this place." Byrinius said in a grave and urgent tone.

"Never! I will not run when my Queen's lands are in danger. I am no coward." Kell bellowed, outrage in his voice.

"Bravery in the face of such a monster is suicide," Byrinius said calmly. "The power behind Visalth is cunning, and so you must be just as crafty. Ashrune may be a noble weapon but even with the might of a Titan behind, it would barely scratch the creature's skull before you were impaled. You need something far mightier, and to find such a thing you need help that is beyond simple magic. You need an Angel."

Check out the rest of the story in book or audio book format on my website: www.LordHartRules.com

My Other Books and Audio Books

THE ANGEL'S BLESSING
HOLY PALADIN'S QUEST
BLAINE HART

SPELL MASTER
WIZARD'S QUEST
BLAINE HART

Blaine Hart
The Bard's Tale
A Mysterious Journey

THE SANDS OF TIME
THE ANGEL'S BLESSING
BLAINE HART

For A Special Treat, check out my
<u>AUDIO BOOKS</u>

Thanks for reading!

If you enjoyed this book a nice review would be greatly appreciated.

Check Out all My Books and Audio Books at:
www.LordHartRules.com

www.ingramcontent.com/pod-product-compliance
Lightning Source LLC
Chambersburg PA
CBHW082103090726

47910CB00008B/2575